FAIRYTALE FUCKERY

Featuring

FAIRYTALE FUCKERY

FAIRYTALE FUCKERY

This book is for entertainment purposes only.

Library of Congress Control Number: 2024938455

Printed in United States of America

ISBN: 9798894670027

TABLE OF CONTENTS

THE MUSHROOM PRINCESS...BERT LESTRANGE...5

NEVER ENOUGH...CODY MATTHEWS...29

BLOOD WHITE...K.L.RASMUSSEN...51

WUNDERLAND...ANDY HOLBERRY...65

THE SIREN'S CURSE...CARIETTA DORSCH...87

TOYMAKER...DEVIN CABRERA...103

PLAGUE BRINGER: DARK FAIRTYTALE...L.W. YOUNG...119

GOLDIE AND THE WOLF...BILL FREAS...141

EDGAR AND THE FAIRY...SUSAN E. ROGERS...165

DUCK...DAVID E. ANDERSON...173

THE CLOCKWORK CHILDREN...MARIE LESTRANGE...187

THE MUSHROOM PRINCESS

Bert Lestrange

Once upon a time, there was a magical king-dom known far and wide for its benevo-lent King, industrious Queen, and joyous people. Luminaria was a flourishing land of seemingly endless abundance and prosperity.

But that was long, long ago in a world nearly forgotten.

The kingdom had since withered beneath a bleak curse. Once verdant fields became a scarred wasteland of barren wombs beneath an eternal, soulless twilight sky. Its people were gaunt, starving husks bound to a life of agony within the realm's borders. Trade with outside lands died overnight as sorrow and despair had replaced gold and silver as their currency. Among all the things stolen by this dark magic, the cruelest was the mercy of death.

Princess Khalida was no exception. She endured the weight of her people's suffering with every step of her own. Even as a child, she'd known only endless hunger and crushing fatigue. Her heart ached seeing her own mirrored torment in the skeletal forms and hollow eyes of her people. In her lifetime, no one in Luminaria had known the comfort of a full stomach or the peace of restful sleep. She'd never experienced anything else.

King Evergreen, her father, was slowly driven to madness by his impotence to protect his kingdom and the loss of his Queen. She'd passed during Khalida's birth. That would prove a blessing as the endless hunger began soon after.

Food offered nothing of satiety, and some even filled their bellies with stones, but nothing helped. Many called to Death, praying to be taken away, but Death had gone deaf. Their own attempts only added new suffering as even grievous wounds, drowning, and burning refused to separate body from spirit. Mutilated cadavers carried their own wailing heads. Society devolved into a starving, shambling corpse.

Like a mushroom, Princess Khalida ruled a diseased, rotting kingdom.

Khalida spent her days scouring the kingdom for any solution, no matter how desperate. She prayed to every god and demon, attempted every spell and ritual, until only one dim hope remained. She would need to seek out the source and put an end to it herself.

The Deadlands weren't so different from her kingdom, a haunted, corpse-littered swamp the dread witch Grestel called home. In every credible history, she had cursed Luminaria by manifesting her hatred in the form of darkest magic.

Knowing this journey to be hers alone, Khalida gathered what useful trinkets she could. A mystical sword of legend, said to devour magic, sat ready on her hip. Before it faded entirely, the wizards and sorceresses of the nation came together and poured their combined magic into a pair of silver coins, as silver was touted to be immune to evil. She placed one in each pocket.

Finally, she took up a handkerchief with three drops of her mother's blood. Before the Queen's death, she was known as a powerful enchantress and created the token as a protective charm for the daughter still in her womb.

The swamp proved a nightmare incarnate. It was filled with twisted, grotesque trees that reached for Khalida with thorny branches. An oppressive, ever-present fog stank of rot and decay. Skeletal remains mocked her from beneath fetid waters and where they hung in trees. Toads and toadstools encouraged her onward, whispering for her to go deeper.

As she ventured deeper, she came to the first true challenge. A mossy creature lumbered from the filthy morass with eyes that burned like hot embers. Its gnarled limbs and snarling maw spoke of the same hunger that plagued her people. She drew the sword, but before she could strike, it lunged.

But rather than fangs against her flesh, she felt only cold ash and smoke as the thing dissipated to dust. The handkerchief pulsed protective energy from her pocket, and she noticed, to her dismay, that one of the crimson drops was gone.

Khalida pressed on with a heavy heart, knowing that her mother's protective magic would wane all too soon.

The second beast erupted from a shadowy mass of vines, larger than the first, with many sharp claws and long clutching arms that told of her people's ever-growing desperation and emaciation. She didn't bother with the sword, instead holding the handkerchief out like a shield. Her hand shook as the second droplet fell, and the creature simultaneously burst into mist. Once more, she was saved by her mother's protective magic.

A third and final abomination caught her by surprise. Many heads lashed out all at once from sickly, serpentine bodies. Each had dead, empty sockets that mirrored her own emptiness. Their luminescent scales glowed faintly with malice even as row after row of fangs dripped wicked venom. The sword flashed even in the twilight, severing three necks, but dozens more struck true with blinding speed. As the final drop of blood faded, so did her protection. The hydra erupted into swirling dust.

Now, utterly vulnerable, she held the magic sword at the ready and slashed wildly at anything even remotely threatening. That proved unnecessary as she reached the dark heart of the Deadlands. A path of bone, stick, and stone wound through the marsh to a hut made entirely of crow feathers and sinewy twine. As if in contemplation of a proper murder, individual crows glared down from the moss-bearded trees above.

Khalida stared at them, brandishing her blade, and when her attention returned to the hut, she saw Grestel. There could be no mistaking the witch's identity. Her eerie elegance was in stark contrast to the ugliness of her domain. Though her robes were tattered scraps of stitched garments, her feminine shape was evident. Long, golden curls dripped down to her hips. But, burning through the ageless beauty, her eyes were filled with ancient pain, unrelenting spite, and obvious recognition.

"Princess Khalida." Her voice was silky honey laced with caustic venom. "Have you come to pay for your father's betrayal?"

Khalida raised the sword in trembling hands before falling to her knees. "I come to beg forgiveness on behalf of my father, myself, and my people. Your terrible power has decimated our kingdom. We suffer endlessly and even death's reprieve remains an elusive dream. What must I do to lift this curse? What price must be paid for Father's debt? Name anything, and it's yours."

"Rise, girl. There's no need to grovel. I know what you've endured. Come, share tea with me, and learn the reason for your torment. Afterwards, we will discuss the fare of your kingdom's freedom."

Grestel placed a surprisingly tender hand on Khalida's shoulder, bidding her to rise. If she feared the blade, she didn't reveal it.

With a bitter smile, the witch served the princess a tea of sweet and spicy herbs: ginger, cinnamon, clove, and allspice.

"It may astonish you to know that your father and I were once desperately in love. We passed years whispering sweet nothings and staring into one another's eyes. When he came of age and it was time to marry, he shattered my heart. I wasn't his only lover, and his mistress proved fertile ground for his recklessly sewn seed. Even as he whispered those crushing words, you were growing in your mother's belly. A talented enchantress, lovely beyond compare, a sweet and gentle girl too innocent and naïve to understand the mistakes she had made. The fault of blame lay not with her, but with him. Had I not fallen for the same fool?"

She took a long sip of tea, wistfully remembering, then refilled her mug.

"Your father spurned me for her. All men think with their cocks, and Autumn was more beautiful than me, younger, kinder, and willing to be molded into his perfect little subservient bride. But some of it was honor and duty, and you were in her womb, not mine. Knowing I wouldn't be content with this marriage, he gathered his mages and banished me to the Deadlands. That was a final straw which deserved retribution. I wanted to hurt him. To wound him so deeply that he would never forget the pain he caused me, nor would his kingdom. It wasn't enough to ruin his life; I wanted to desecrate his legacy. So, I sacrificed my own ability to bear children to curse his. The curse isn't on the land or even the king, my dear, but on you."

Grestel prodded Khalida's ribs with a long, graceful finger.

"On me? What do you mean?" The princess's heart thundered in her ears.

The witch continued, eyes glittering with malevolence. "There is only one true way to lift the curse. It's a powerful, ancient spell. You must spill your own blood onto the sacred Juniper tree. Take your life. Trade it to save your people, or their pain will last until the sun finally dies and consumes everything."

Khalida's face went milk-pale, and tears welled in her eyes. "Is this the only way? Surely another path exists?"

Grestel sighed, draining her mug and setting it aside.

"If you lack the courage to properly satisfy your father's debt, then you must break the magic with your own hand. The sacred Juniper is the key to all powerful spells in this region. It is the physical manifestation marking where two leylines of power converge. It was and is a necessary component for both your curse and my magical exile. I intended to destroy it years back to end my imprisonment from this stinking, rotting place. If that meant ending your curse, then so be it. But I couldn't touch so much as a needle. It's a sacred plant in a sacred place. I can't pass its barrier because my heart is impure. You, however, have no such limitations."

Khalida's blood froze in her veins. "Where would I find this tree?"

"You'll need a spirit guide." She grinned wickedly. "Can you pay for the service? Would you do what is necessary to save your people, even knowing it would free me?"

The princess took out the two silver coins, holding them out for inspection. "Is this enough? I will do anything."

"The spirit will take its toll. Yes, that will be enough. Continue the journey until you reach an impassable depth of dark water. The crimson ferryman will find you soon after."

Khalida steeled her resolve. "Then that is what will be done."

She turned to leave, but Grestel tugged her shoulder for one last word of wisdom.

"Kill the Juniper tree, but do not take anything from it, berry, needle, or bark. The consequences of disobedience are dire. This is your only warning. Now go and rectify the sins of your father."

The princess, determined to save her kingdom, walked for hours and noticed only an otherworldly silence. No bird nor bug nor beast made any sound at all. No wind rustled so much as a leaf or stirred the murk's surface. Eventually, she found the deep water and waited.

Only a few minutes passed before a small boat of rotting wood appeared. At its long, iron pole stood a spectral creature beneath a blood-stained cloak that hid its eyes. Somewhere between wolf and man, the figure held out a clawed hand with long fingers.

"Toll?" it wheezed.

Khalida placed both coins in its palm and the ferryman nodded for her to join him.

Rasping, it asked, "Where would you go?"

"To the sacred Juniper tree," she answered.

It nodded. "The tree of life."

And their slow journey began. It used its pole to propel them along the treacherous waters without a word. Hundreds of blue flamed balls danced across the water, silently begging her to join them and promising riches beyond knowing. She did not answer the call but watched them go.

"What is the tree of life? What is its purpose?" She asked to pass the time.

The lupine spirit answered. "It is a place of great power. The tree embodies white magic; healing, protection, and rebirth. Its bark is indestructible armor, its berries cure any ailment, its roots can revive the dead, and its needles are pure silver."

"It has so many wonderful benefits; why can't one take from the tree?" The princess asked.

The ferryman shook its head. "There is no law against it, mortal, moral, or mystical. The tree is open to all and welcomes any with a pure heart."

Upon reaching the island, Khalida found a verdant paradise, a stark contrast to the desolation of her own homeland and the swamp itself.

The sacred Juniper tree stood at the center, radiating its own faint white light. Its bark and needles gleamed, and the berries were a lustrous, glowing blue. Hunger gnawed at her very soul upon seeing the berries, clawing at her resolve. But she was here to lift the curse. She wept over the tree's beauty and what must be done.

As she reached for the magic sword, desperation and hunger shattered her discipline. She dropped the blade, taking a handful of berries to stuff in her mouth. The sweet fruit burst with flavor, and a warm wave of vitality washed over her. For the first time in her life, Princess Khalida felt whole, healthy, and satisfied. It magically transformed her body from an emaciated husk to the soft, curvaceous figure of a princess. An umbra of darkest shadow lifted from her shoulders. She wept again, but this time with joy.

When no terrible calamity followed, she stuffed her pockets with the berries, intending to give them to everyone she passed on the journey home. Emboldened, she took from the bark, planning to make her father an amulet to protect his heart. The needles indeed proved to be pure silver, and she took a bough to pay the ferryman for her return passage.

But, with nothing left to do, she weighed her options. If she spilled her blood, the curse would lift, but she would never see what followed or experience this life free of ravenous hunger and anguished sorrow. If she killed the tree, Grestel would be free, and the beautiful tree would be no more. But she had the berries and would plant it anew. Give it a new life in the center of her castle's garden, as it would grant her kingdom a new life and a better place to live.

She should sacrifice herself, but having tasted health and happiness, she found herself unwilling to let it go. With a heavy heart, she made the decision.

Raising the blade, Khalida stabbed it deep into the tree's heart. It shuddered and let out a soul-wrenching scream of agony that echoed until the sword drank the very last of its magic. In her hands, it rusted and shattered. The sacred Juniper tree withered to a grey shrivel, its light gone forever. In her pockets, the berries melted into black tar. The silver needles dropped from the lifeless bough.

Realizing the gravity of her mistake, she gathered the needles and ran to the waiting spirit. It took them as payment but shook its head in disappointment at what she'd done. It ignored her attempts at conversation and left the moment its task was completed.

She found Grestel tending a cooking fire.

"You are no different than your father. Taking the easy route over the proper one." The witch sneered. "I see you've eaten the fruit. You look well, Princess. By your hand, the curse is lifted, and I am free. Go enjoy the spoils of your actions. We will speak again soon enough."

And with that, the dread witch Grestel burst into a cloud of black crows and flew into the night.

Guilt battled with pride as she walked from the Deadlands. She noticed, suddenly, that the marsh had become a peaceful forest. Natural life returned to the Deadlands, and the sky above lightened with the sun's rays which she'd never seen. It was like incorporeal gold drifting to the earth.

Hope bloomed and with a light heart, she skipped all the way back to her Kingdom.

Yet, upon her return, hope was corrupted by horror. The air was thick with death and decay. True death, rather than the usual lifelessness. Her people lay where they'd fallen, rotting in the sun without spirit to animate them. Panic and fear hastened her footsteps as she ran to the throne room, to her father. His corpse was among the dead as crows plucked meat and eyeballs. The princess collapsed into sobs atop her former father's fetid form.

She didn't notice the crows gathering into a murder or Grestel's form emerging from it.

"Foolish girl. Look what you've done." The witch cackled.

Princess Khalida wept as she answered. "What have I done? This is your devilry, witch. You tricked me!"

Her cruel smirk was salt in the wound. "I did nothing of the sort. Had you sacrificed yourself, the curse would be broken with your death. But the sacred Juniper tree would have resurrected you from your blood. By eating the berries, you gained immortality. The necessary sacrifice would no longer be possible. By taking the bark, you stole its protection from your blade. Taking its silver needles revealed your own greed. You have doomed your kingdom and have eternity to mourn your mistakes."

"No! It can't be..." The princess whispered, even as the crushing weight of truth crashed down on her.

Grestel's eyes glittered with newfound power. "Thank you for breaking my chains. I am free to walk the world once more, and my power is returned. Good-bye, Princess. Enjoy a long, long life by your wicked father's side."

Khalida stood, reaching for a sword that no longer existed.

With a wave of her hand, Grestel cracked the earth and a fissure appeared beneath the princess's feet. She tumbled down and down and down. At the bottom, she shrieked at the agony of mangled limbs and shattered bones.

Crows cawed above and a weight crashed down, splatting beside her. It was the body of her father. Then another, and another. Crows numbering in the millions gathered her dead kingdom and dropped them down atop her head until she was buried in the putrid flesh of her beloved people.

The earth shuddered and closed around her. There she was trapped, left to endure an eternity of regret and sorrow, lamenting her own greed and selfishness until the end of time. Maggots would wriggle against her body, filling her mouth, eyes, and nose. Mushrooms would sprout from her flesh, and she would scream into the uncaring void.

And so it was that Princess Khalida suffered endlessly ever after.

Bert Lestrange's works include various degrees of Horror, Fantasy, Weird Fiction, and, occasionally, unadulterated Smut. He is the husband of Marie Lestrange, world traveler, and self-proclaimed foodie— though he has a weakness for gast station chilli dogs. He and his family's roots spiderweb across the mountains of East Tennessee. Caregiver, father, and proud ally. Nicest asshole you'll ever meet.

NEVER ENOUGH

Cody Matthews

My name is Rapunzel, Maxine Rapunzel. January 12, 2024. My life didn't go as planned. And it started after my mom died. When I took on the challenge of keeping my mom's death a secret, staying in the house until I could find my true lover to move in with. I lived in a castle out in the middle of nowhere, so I thought this should be easy, but it wasn't long until I started running out of food—two weeks, to be exact.

I've never had to deal with the maintenance of the house, nor handle any responsibilities, mainly because my mom did all that for me. Gave me every-thing I ever wanted: my pink silk dress, my king-sized bed with a white ruffle princess canopy, my collection of 200 high heels and diamond slippers, my red mystic topaz diamond ring my mom dug up and crafted for me, and then my maid that she paid to do all my dishes and chores so I didn't have to.

This was my life as far as I can remember.

But now, since I was on my own, I was very un-certain whether or not I'd survive, not to mention I had no real skills, so the chances of me providing for my-self was slim to none. I couldn't cook anything, not without hurting myself or burning the food, and getting close to a fire scared me, so cooking something over the fireplace was out of the question.

I hated feeding myself because I'd drop every-thing I picked up. Like the first morning after my mom died, I made myself a bowl of cereal, dropping two of my favorite bowls and breaking them. "Grrrrrr! Stupid! Stupid!" I then grabbed one of my mom's bowls, poured the cereal inside, then grabbed the milk, knocking into the counter and dropping it on the floor, the milk exploding in every direction. "Grrrrrrrrrr!"

For months I would do this. It was the main reason I ran out of food so quickly. But two months after my mother's death, I decided to take the six-mile trot into town, something my mother never let me do.

I entered a place called "Skid Row," apparently a bar, where I sat on a stool, smiling at people. I've always had a hard time socializing, mainly because I never talked to anyone but myself, not even with my mother, who only gave me commands, so I never had a real conversation before.

Nevertheless, that all changed when Grady Gibson approached me, a tall man with combed-over hair that was smooth and brown, and perfectly groomed facial hair. He stood straight with a half-smile, which was so infectious you forgot he wasn't really smiling. We shared a gaze that made me feel like I had to laugh, but also relaxed me. I'd never felt this way before.

"Can I buy you a drink?" asked Grady, "Mrzzzzzz—"

I kept eye contact, but sat there with furrowed eyebrows and a smile.

He sighed. "What's your name?" Grady inquired with slight vexation.

"O, Rapunzel. It's Rapunzel. Sorry." I cleared my throat.

He turned to the bartender. "Two bloody marys, please!" He had the smoothest and deepest voice I've ever heard, not the way you're probably thinking. His voice almost had a whisper to it, a whisper of reassurance. He had a dance-like motion to his hand gestures and head movement when he talked.

The bartender placed two highball glasses, into which he poured half a glass of tomato juice, two spoons of lemon juice, and vodka, filling the rest of the glasses.

Of course, I had no idea what was mixed in them.

Grady took a sip and turned to me. "I have a question." He repositioned himself in his seat.

I sipped on my drink with a scrunched up face. "Mmm, Hmm," I answered.

He scooted his chair closer. I glanced at him from my peripheral, kind of giddy.

"What do you think about getting married?" he asked.

"Mmmm, I don't know. We don't really know each other yet."

"Are you looking to get married?"

I swallowed and cleared my throat. His questions had an effect on me. They caused me to question my options, but also— I never wanted to say no— but I'm not trying to be mean about it either. I did and still love him.

I smiled. "Yeah. Eventually," I said, tucking my

hair behind my right ear.

We talked about marriage, what to name our kids, hobbies, and future plans. Staying in the bar from 4 pm to 2 am, I had the best moments of my life. The conversation was nothing I've ever had before, full of energy, making me feel really good.

I felt safe and loved around him. He listened to everything I said, letting me talk, as he listened with his head tilted. I couldn't get enough of his attention, and never wanted to leave his side. I've never felt THIS welcome around a man before, and he was extremely charming, being so animated when he talked, describing a moment he fought a burglar in his house, saving his little cousin, Gina May, by choking him out with a guitar string.

He had a way of smiling with his eyes, which made him so engaging to talk to. I always had to fight the urge to smile while I was around him, and he always had the relaxing smell of eucalyptus on his clothes.

Before I knew it, we were at his house.

"You said you eventually want to get married, right?" he inquired, his eyes glistening with a subtle smile.

I had a surge of ebullience. I wanted to say what he wanted me to say, the feeling consuming me. Could I say no, though? That would be mean for me to do. He would never talk to me again, and I would have to go back to the castle. And the moments with him felt so good, and he made me feel so important; any answer I gave him was whatever he wanted. I want this to last.

My face got warm. I looked down with a weird numbness to my cheeks, unable to control my smile.

"I mean, I want to get married someday," I said, looking down and fiddling with my dress.

His eyes stayed on me. I wasn't on stage, but I felt like I was. Come to think about it, he was studying me.

He said, "What about now? Would you want to get married NOW?"

I crossed my arms. "Yeah, I guess so."

Is this normal? We'd only been talking for five or six hours. How are we talking about marriage already? Isn't it a bit soon?

Me and Grady spent the whole next day watching movies and playing board games. While watching Carter's Son, I accidentally spilled my coke on him while reaching for the blankets, and that really upset him, to the point he was answering me with "sure" and "I don't know" all day.

I ignored it, thinking it was just a moment. But as we were playing board games, he sat completely silent the whole time…and something about his irate eyes being wide and bulging made me apprehensive, and it wasn't just his eyes. The way he would touch his side pockets, which had a rectangular cylinder object inside, touching and feeling it every three minutes or so. At this point, it was my turn to move,

"Are you upset? Is that why you're not playing the game?" he snapped.

"Ummm, I—"

"We don't have to play. Let's just go get something to eat. I don't want to argue with you."

We drove to get some lunch, and his ominous charades got morrrrrrrre—specific; while driving on a road with a solid yellow line, he would—at what felt like planned times—turn into oncoming traffic, almost hitting an eight-wheeler truck the second time.

After the distressing car ride, we walked into a Dizzy Weasel's pizza place, where we ordered some food. As we were making our way to a table, I tripped on something, sending me into the ground on top of my food.

For a moment everything was a haze, hearing

other customer's voices echo around me. I came to and saw Grady walking to a table in the back, turning back to me with a look of confusion and frustration, mouthing to me, "What the fuck are you doing?" My favorite pink t-shirt was covered in red sauce, the cheese all over my face and hair.

Grady walked over and grabbed me by the arm, hoisting me on my feet. "Are you upset? Is that why you're embarrassing me? Huh?" he thundered.

I froze in place with a quiet, "I'm sorry, I'm sorry." Thinking back on it, why was I apologizing to him?

Once we got back to the car, he hit the steering wheel, "Why do you do this to me? First you get upset with me for asking about marriage, and now we're about to get married, and this is how you treat me? I put so much time and energy into you, Rapunzel! Just because you're miserable, doesn't mean you have to make me miserable, too!"

I sat there with my head buzzing and my body feeling stiff and numb.

"Are you just gonna sit there?" he asked. "Or are you gonna apologize for humiliating me in public?"

There were no thoughts in my head; I was paralyzed with a weird numbness, and when I opened my mouth to say something—

"Hello? Do you even freaking care?" he snapped and interrupted.

I opened my mouth again.

"Are you THAT stupid?" he admonished. "Can you not do anything for yourself? How pathetic! No wonder you're treated like crap!"

Am I not a good girlfriend? What can I do to fix this? We're so close now, and he makes me feel so good. I don't want to make this worse.

Maybe I was just intimidated by his take-charge nature. I loved him for wanting the best for me. That's why he was so hard on me.

The next day. I woke up to him throwing a white dress at me.

"Put this on," he ordered. "We have a wedding today, unless you forgot that, too. You said you wanted to get married someday, nodding yes when I asked you about today! Does our marriage even matter to you?"

I lifted my head from my pillow, rubbing my eyes.

"Rapunzel?" he yelled in a drawn-out, demanding voice, then, "Rapunzellll!" The way he yelled this… I don't know. It haunted me.

I kicked the covers back. "What? What?"

He bent down with a sharp gaze, dark circles around his eyes, standing completely still, his face somehow going more and more lifeless the longer he stared at me. *Do what he says*, I thought. *He's just upset.*

Yet this seemed really personal, like it was aimed at me. But because I wanted this to work out, I continued making eye contact. I stood up, straightened my back, and began to put on my dress.

At my parents' church, Luther Green Baptist Church, he and I stood in an empty room, me with my white dress on and him in his tux. The fluorescent lights were all flickering. Scanning around, I saw nothing but picture frames of God paintings on the wall. I rubbed my forearms, looking down. He was still upset. I glanced at him from my peripheral,

"Are you okay? Hello?" I asked in a soft quiet voice. He stood with his hands by his sides, motionless.

What happened? Why was he acting like this? The piano music played outside. Grady put his hands out next to mine, in which I locked my hand with his. His hands were warm, but with no energy or presence. We both made our way down the aisle.

"Rapunzellll!!!" Grady yelled— but when I turned to Grady, he wasn't looking at me or talking. It sounded like it came from afar, but also close by.

We continued walking down the aisle. Some people in the back pews were smiling at Grady, while my family members were concerned in the front, looking away the minute we met eyes. The lights were on, but the room looked dim, dim in a way where it almost felt like a dream. The lighting in the room gave everything a bright yellow look.

What's going on? Did I even wake up this morning?

We got up to the stage of the church. Grady and I were facing each other, reaching out, and locking our hands together. I couldn't break away from how dim the room appeared, and how distant everything felt. I tried to let one of my hands loose from Grady's, but he wouldn't let go; so instead, I scratched my leg with one of my high-heel shoes to keep myself from freaking out. There was talking going on, yet it sounded like it was coming from somewhere else.

"Miss Rapunzel," echoed the distant voice,

"Miss Rapunzel?" The priest thundered louder than usual. I snapped back with cold sweats, "Yes? Yes?"

The priest stared at me with a pause, "Do you accept Mister Gibson for as long as you both shall live, through life or death?" The feeling of the room being dim and everything being distant continued to loom.

"I do. I do," I sputtered.

I didn't hear what else he said. All I remember is Grady leaning in to kiss me and my family cheering. Grady disappeared right after our kiss. Different unknown people approached and shook my hand,

"Congratulations, Rapunzel!" said an older man in a black suit, red tie, and white hair.

I stood in place on stage. Why was Grady acting weird? Why did I feel like I'm not doing something? And what was I supposed to do? Me and Grady loved each other, right?

After 30 minutes, Grady approached me making no eye contact, walking past me like I didn't exist. I kept my eyes on him, then waved. Nothing.

When we got back to his place, Grady locked himself in his room. After sitting on the couch for thirty minutes, I mustered the courage to knock on the door.

"Grady?" I bashfully inquired, my knocks perhaps not even loud enough to be heard… Nothing. My hands frozen by my chest, both folded, gripping my hands tighter as my eyes darted back and forth, gazing at the ground. My grip softened, and tightened, softened, and tightened.

I was barely breathing, only taking small breaths every other minute, and my chest felt heavy.

His door opened with a loud click-like metal noise, for some reason making me jump. He wandered out of his room— it's ink dark. What the— he walked past me like I wasn't there.

"Are you gonna talk to me? What did I do?"

He got himself a bowl of cereal.

"Can I do something? You've been like this for

two days now."

Grady wandered back to his room, the door echoing shut.

The next day, I thought it couldn't get worse. But the second he woke up, he had his laptop with a website on the screen called "Moore's Fun." It had a picture of a woman in provocative clothing, on her hands and knees. Tons of images of other naked women, videos included. Though I was consumed with profound rage, for some reason I still tried to make him feel good again. Offering him food, drinks, movies—but the one thing that seemed to intrigue him was…sex.

Next thing I know I'm tied to the bedpost with rope, after agreeing to do it his way. I thought it was odd, and creeped me out a bit, but went with it because I was ready for him to be happy again. Granted, the sex was more of him screaming and threatening me, right after wrapping both sets of fingers around my neck, squeezing for what felt like an hour, though it was only a minute or two. Squeezing a little harder before stopping for a drink. He was smiling and happy afterwards.

"You wanna go out for a wedding dinner?" he inquired in a soft tone with a serene smile.

"Isn't it a little late for that?" I joked with a nervous chuckle.

His face went from a serene infectious smile to less than a half smile with a wide look in his eyes that had an uncanny effect on them. He fixated on me a little longer than I was comfortable with, making me freeze up. The silence was deafening along with the ringing in my ears, which got louder and louder.

"Are you o—"

He interrupted, "Do you like making me uncomfortable?"

"Wha—"

"Do you like making me uncomfortable? Because you've been nothing but distant with me since the wedding, and I'm starting to wonder if marrying you was a good idea."

I stood there in disbelief. I didn't know I was making him uncomfortable. Was that why he was quiet with me? But he'd been distant with me too… Right? I mean, come to think about it, I was just standing there at the wedding acting weird. Just standing there thinking to myself that the room was dim and distant-feeling… Maybe I am the one causing the problems.

"It was a good idea. I'm sorry, I—"

He interrupted again, saying, "What the hell does sorry do? You've been distant with me, then nagged at me about not talking to you."

I remember when I first met him, I don't think I remember talking to him much. Is that what he meant? Should I have talked to him more at the beginning? Or is it because I'm not talking to him now?

"Rapunzel?" His voice demanded in a loud, drawn-out way, "Rapunzel?"

I blinked rapidly and shook my head. "Yes, yes, what is it? What?"

"I'm done! You're socially stupid, you know that? You need to be more competent and stop being so distant with everyone around you!" he said, striding out the door.

He never came back. I was back in a similar position I'd been in before. But this time at his apartment. I tried to make the food in the pantries last as long as possible, but by the end of the second week I was on the last pieces of bologna and bread, and unable to stop thinking about Grady.

I got to the point where I was crying every second of every day, thinking if I was more caring, competent, and social. I would get him back. Maybe it was because I wasn't like him. Because I heard that you're supposed to compromise with your partner. I should've compromised with him more. I should've been more aware of his needs. I'll never forgive myself for the way I acted at our wedding… Maybe there's something wrong with me.

But luckily, I found another man at the same bar three days later, and we talked for hours before going to his place. This time…I'm gonna make it work. I still want Grady back, though.

I love you, Grady.

I'm Cody Matthews! I didn't always start with writing books, in fact, my dream was to become a script writer for mature cartoons on tv: like the simpsons and south park. A lot of my stories for these scripts I practiced writing were full of dark humor, whether if that was a younger sister killing people and stealing her mom's credit cards to go to a theme park; or if that was a mom character losing her mind, then starting a crappy comedy special on netflix. This is the stuff I wrote. It wasn't until later that my biological mom suggested writing books or short stories, something I didn't seriously consider, just because I was DEAD set on writing tv scripts. Granted, I had short stories in mind that I wanted to write. One of them was a magician that psychologically torments two siblings after they discover and open a dead magician's magic kit. Magicians still freak me out! Glad I'm not these kids! Anyways. Skip ahead. Several months ago, while prolifically posting on a FB horror story group, just seeing what kind of criticism I could get from my stories, and the next thing I knew, I was buying a book on amazon containing dozens of short stories by talented aspiring authors, including myself.

BLOOD WHITE

K.L. RASMUSSEN

Traipsing between the freshly fallen bodies and pooling blood, Snow White trembles at seeing the destruction around her once strong and healthy kingdom, now reaped of its former glory by the Queen's vanity. Soldiers that had once fought beside her father lay slain and decapitated, their heads plunged on spikes in front of the gate.

Just like the Huntsman.

Snow shudders at the thought of his mutilated body and severed head, which stood as a warning for anyone who tried to aid Snow White from evading her capture.

Ash falls from the sky. The ebony tree her mother was most fond of sits crumbling and burnt from the root. Its once-strong branches are now broken and cut for lumber for the Queen's death machines. Her heart was as black as coal, if she ever had one.

I shouldn't have come here, Snow thinks. She could be living her happily-ever-after right now, but instead, she begged and pleaded to be brought here.

Looking around, Snow knows that it is hopeless. What does she have to reclaim? All that's left is rubble and fragments of her past—beyond repair.

She could start fresh with the prince in his kingdom and leave this nightmare behind. Everything her father had given to protect this kingdom was now reduced to rubble and death. The bodies of the valiant men who fought alongside her father now lay strewn about, shredded to pieces.

Snow White chokes back a mixture of tears and disgust as she notices a few fingers and toes in her path. The rancid smell of burnt flesh and decay ensnares them, using their cloaks to cover their faces as they pass.

She has half a mind to turn away and leave this place behind, as she'd intended before. She has no idea what horrors lay for her inside the castle. Behind her, she feels her prince with his unwavering support.

Just as it has been since he found her in the glass coffin.

"What's wrong?" he asks.

"Everything."

She continues forward with brevity, her dress tearing as she steps on shards of glass and fragmented sheetrock. But her dress is the least of her worries as she passes through the broken ebony front doors to the entrance hall.

What will happen when she finds it?

What enchanting treachery the Queen has. Wickedness and vanity had poisoned her heart and stained the castle walls with horrors beyond comprehension. Wooden chairs and tables splintered in half. Thick stone walls were blown apart. Death hung like curtains. Skinned and tanned like cattle hide, leathered human skin decorated the walls as if the Queen had taken up quilting the villagers in her free time.

That sick fucking bitch.

Taking what is left of the crumbling grand staircase, Snow White shudders to think what they will find in the rooms above. The prince sticks close to catch Snow in case she falls.

It feels like a lifetime since Snow has walked these halls. And nothing is how she remembers it before. She's not even sure which door leads to her bed-chambers anymore. Before Snow had escaped, she was restricted to her bedchambers, the courtyard, and any of the servants' quarters, which are now barren of any life.

The rest belonged to Her Majesty, the Queen. What darkness lurks behind each heavy ebony door? Each of the brass doorknobs has rusted with decay or fallen to the stone floor.

Snow does not dare reach for any of them; she does not want to know, yet she feels guilty for not bearing the weight of the Queen's cruelty. Worried that some poor soul was left to die, Snow decides they must clear the castle of any dangers.

Taking a step towards the first door in the corridor, Snow's hand trembles as she reaches for the door handle; her prince wields his sword, ready for whatever gruesome danger lurks beyond. Snow turns the handle and pushes the door—it creaks open, mimicking the shrieks of something supernatural and cursed. Yet the room is unoccupied. Draped with sheets and dust, it had been left unused for some time.

Snow sighs in relief, scolding herself for getting so worked up over nothing. Certainly, if something alive and dangerous here remained, it would make itself known.

She signals to her prince that there is no danger and they push forward, passing grand portraits that have been ripped to shreds, fragments of stone walls still crumble as the castle shifts, adjusting to a new state of decay.

The prince holds Snow White tight, feeling her want to crumble along with it. Her childhood home is like a wilted rose, but he will not let his future Queen fall apart. He's only just rescued her, saved her from an eternity of slumber.

Despite his efforts, she insisted on coming here, to see what was left of her father's kingdom. Hoping to end this petty feud once and for all.

But the bitch is nowhere to be seen. That's when she's most dangerous.

Snow doesn't know, but if the old crone lays a hand on her, he will drive her through with his sword.

The prince has it all planned. He's won the fairest in the land. She's all his. He cannot lose her when he has come so far.

He wasn't sure if he'd see her again, let alone if he would be the one to claim her as his. He was certain he'd startled her that day he came upon her in the garden. He'd heard the sweetest voice singing and humming and then stumbled upon the most breathtaking woman he'd ever laid eyes upon. Hair as black as the coal mined by the kingdom's dwarves, lips as red as blood, and skin so fair and white he feared it would break like porcelain. He wondered what it would be like to kiss and bite those red lips, to pull her ebony hair back as he bent her over the balcony for the entire kingdom to see.

But Snow was anything but fragile, and the Prince knew this. But no matter how tough she may seem, he was in for an uphill battle against her inner demons.

With his hand on the hilt of his sword, he continues to follow her down the corridor of the castle's South Wing, where the Queen had kept her domain of dark secrets.

The glow of the moonlight cast a halo on the abandoned bed chambers, the moonbeams bouncing off the elaborate mirror hanging in the air by invisible threads—dark magic.

Snow takes a step towards it, but the Prince holds her back.

"Snow, it's not worth it. It twisted and warped the Queen's mind. I don't want the same becoming of you."

"Her mind was twisted, to begin with. I need answers," Snow says defiantly, pulling his hand away.

The prince gulps but follows behind. *Through thick and thin*, he reminds himself.

Snow wanders toward the mirror as if it calls to her in a way that the Prince does not understand, until he hears, "You think you're worthy of the fairest in the land, huh, pretty boy?"

"Who the fuck said that?" the prince yells, ready to grab Snow and run. He saved his princess; he did what he had to, what he set out to do from the very moment he saw her.

"I have news for you," the voice says. "You're nothing. She could do so much better than you. You're just some punk that happened upon a helpless girl in the woods. Does she know what you were doing before you approached her?" The voice hisses in his ear like a snake coaxing him into the forbidden fruit. But he mustn't take the bait.

"No! It was a true love's kiss. It's bound to break any spell. You can't fake that shit."

"Who are you talking to?" Snow says, looking at him as if he's gone mad.

The prince stares back, embarrassed to say what he thinks is happening.

"You good?" she asks. "It's just a mirror."

"We should smash it."

"Again, it's just a mirror."

"It's evil, Snow," the prince snaps. "It's taunting me."

Snow jumps. She thinks he's mad, but this mirror was the reason for her near-demise, instructing the Queen with malice and envy, empowering her self-doubt and resentment for the world. Snow wonders what kind of relationship she and her stepmother could have had were it not for the mirror in her life. Was she always this vain? Or did the mirror poison her mind against Snow?

Was there ever a chance that I could have had a mother? Snow ponders. But then she remembers the bitch tried to kill her multiple times, murdered her father, and committed the atrocities left behind.

"You're right." Snow says. "We should smash it."

The prince breathes a sigh of relief. Dark shadows cavort about the room, and a sense of urgency surges through him.

"Would you like to do the honors?" The prince offers his sword to her.

"Why, thank you—such a gentleman," Snow giggles for the first time since their arrival at the castle. *Glad to know she can find humor in a dark place*, the prince thinks with a victorious smile.

She looks so sexy brandishing a sword.

"Does the princess know what a dirty boy you are?" the voice sneers. "What you plan for her when you return to your domain will be revealed?"

No, and she mustn't find out the worst of him.

"Smash it, Snow! What are you waiting for?" the prince urges.

But Snow doesn't move. It's as if she's been turned to stone in front of the mirror, entranced by her reflection.

The mirror has taken Snow back—back to when the Prince laid eyes on her. Watching her from between the bramble and underbrush. Hunting her like wild elk.

How did he find her? Let alone know where she was? The Queen had kept her quite isolated. How did he find her in the first place? The mirror shows the Prince having followed her the whole time—through the woods with the Huntsman, to her finding the Dwarves' cottage in the woods. He was there when the Evil Queen made three attempts on her life. The ribbon, the comb, and the apple. He was there.

All along he knew the Queen's dark disastrous plans that left her in ruin. But how?

The prince pulls her away, throws her over one shoulder, and carries her out the door before the mirror could have a minute's more influence over her—he doesn't know all that was said, but he'd heard enough. The mirror was poisonous. Poison, just like her.

Kicking and screaming, the Prince knew for a fact that Snow had an inkling that their coming together was no accident. Waiting for them, with a menacing glow about her, the Queen—with a smile so wicked, Snow's heart stopped for a second. The prince may as well just carry her to her grave.

Wielding his sword, he holds tight to the princess.

"Well, well, looks like we don't fall far from the tree," her hauntingly sing-song voice carries through the halls and crawls up their spines.

Pointing his sword at her heart as she blocks the exit, the Prince growls, "Step aside, Mother."

K.L Rasmussen is a passionate writer immersed in Victorian and Gothic literature. By day, she shares her love for books as a knowledgeable bookseller at Barnes & Noble. With her feline companion, Minerva, as her muse, she brings stories to life with captivating words and detailed illustrations.

ANDY HOLBERRY

WUNDERLAND

She stumbled down the dark alleyway, the lights from the myriad stores burning shapes into her retinas. The music from a dozen clubs, the yells from corner sequestered pimps selling the flesh they controlled. The whores strutted close by advertising their bodies in tight leather and PVC.

She passed all of this and more as she made her way to the place she wanted to be…needed to be at.

The woman could feel the need crawling like worms through her views, the pulsing beat of a headache pushing at her temples making the lights and sounds so much louder, clearer…more painful in her brain.

She knew the need would be sated soon, the crumpled fifty dollars in her damp pocket almost burning a hole through the fabric. She had managed to steal a radio from a parked car and had pawned it at a well-known spot for the cash.

It would be enough to buy her a couple of days' peace, a chance to leave the world and its horror behind. A chance to fly and soar…even if it were only in her mind.

The cramps hit and she stopped, her hands reaching out to a nearby wall for support. Through blurry eyes, she saw people giving her a wide berth, afraid that she was contagious with a disease.

The pains in her stomach were slowly fading, her intestines becoming more like themselves. She took a deep breath; the air full of food smells, making her insides churn at the thought of food, drug smells…the string heady stench of cheap perfumes.

Getting to her feet again, she continued towards a door she knew well.

There was a neon sign above the red door; the legend had been handwritten in large, swirling red letters. Someone had taken a knife or a blade to the second letter; itt now said 'Wunderland,' and it shone with the light of promise.

She stopped at the threshold and thumped on it once…twice, paused and then a third time. Not much of a secret knock, but then again, the place wasn't much of a secret to start with.

It opened six inches and a scarred black face stared out at her. She couldn't see the eyes where they hid behind dark aviator-like sunglasses.

The man looked at her, his head tilted slightly to one side, a cigarette dangling from one corner of his mouth. His brow furrowed as he looked through the mental drawers in his brain.

"And who…are you?"

She opened her mouth to answer, but the man was quicker.

"Alice? Back again?"

She smiled, the gesture more a grimace, and gulped as she felt the sickness rising. She swallowed loudly and tried again.

"Is…is Hatter here?" She scratched her arms through the thin, torn material of her shirt.

The face looked her up and down, lingering awhile on her breasts, her legs in their tight jeans.

And then it broke out in a smile; even, bright white teeth shining in his dark skin, the grin so wide it seemed to split his face in half.

She felt the need growing stronger as the seconds ticked past.

"You got cash this time? Ain't no freebies here."

She reached down and patted her front pocket where the money sat.

He waited for a minute that stretched to two, she could see her wasted, ragged reflection in the lenses.

Just as she thought he would close the door in her face, it opened and he stepped out of the way. He waved an arm inside the small corridor beyond, exaggerating the movement like a doorman welcoming a VIP.

Alice stepped inside. She walked a dozen steps before she heard the door close and lock behind her.

Alice put a hand to her head and brushed her hair back. It used to be so lush, so silky smooth, now it felt dry as straw. She leaned against the wall for a second, her brain swirling in the silence after the noises from the outside world. Then she felt the need and knew she had to see Hatter soon.

Standing straight, she walked past the first doorway and looked in. Inside the room, in the middle of peeling plasterboard walls and splintered wooden floors was a stained mattress. On it sat identical twins. She knew they were called Dom and Dee. They lived here, or rather, they may as well have. They were always here whenever she turned up for a fix; the building more of a home to them than anywhere else. Where they got their green for their fixes, she didn't know, but they always seemed to be permanently wasted.

They lay there, hands clasped, both flying higher than an aircraft…minds free and in the stratosphere.

She went on, deeper and deeper into the building interior.

The hallway opened up into a main floor that used to be the foyer for a hotel, long since fallen into neglect and disrepair. Threadbare stairs ascended to upper floors. Bodies lay slumped on landings and on floors, wherever there was the slightest bit of space. The bare floors, elegant tiles from an age long past, broken and cracked, were filthy with waste and bile, the smell rising into the air thick and cloying, reaching to the back of the throat. She stepped over a man curled into a ball, his eyes half closed, a used syringe hanging from his arm, an empty baggie on the floor next to a spoon and lighter. He didn't move as she went past.

Alice ignored everyone and shuffled towards a doorway at the far end of the room. She was cold now, her arms wrapped around her body, the need almost held full sway over her body and mind. The door was missing and she stumbled through. The room on the other side was thickly carpeted and she almost fell as the texture changed under her shoes. A single bulb blazed with bright light above, and she had to shield her eyes from the glare.

A desk sat at the far end and a man sat there with his fingers steepled in front of his face. He wore an old top hat. Where it had come from was anyone's guess, but rumor was, it used to be a prop from an old theater. The man smiled, his eyes wide. One pupil was a startling electric blue, the other a deep jade green…the effect was disturbing.

She stopped as she reached the desk, aware that the big black man was standing close behind her. She could feel him just over her shoulder.

"Alice," the man called Hatter said. "How wonderful to see you. You always know just what time to turn up."

He waved a hand at the top of the desk where various plastic bags lay. Small amounts of white and brown powder. Small jars with a multitude of colors and small dirty yellow rocks.

"Would you care to stay for tea?"

She reached into her pocket and pulled out the fifty dollars, a shaking hand reaching across to hand it to him. He took it and dropped it into an open desk drawer. She saw more drugs in there, along with a silver snub-nose .38 revolver, the pearl handle grip catching the light. He leaned forwards and picked up two bags of the brown powder, passing them to her waiting palm. She took them, forcing every part of her not to snatch them from him. She hugged the bags to her, afraid that they would disappear at any moment.

He looked at the man over her shoulder.

"Leroy…would you be so kind as to show Alice here to a quiet room? I'm sure a frequent flier…and a lady, needs some privacy."

The big man took her arm and led her away.

She sat cross-legged on the soiled mattress, its springs digging into her legs and ass, and cooked the heroine on the spoon.

It had been a gift…the spoon. One of a set she had stolen from the family home when she had run away. Alice had kept this last one after selling the rest. A final reminder of who she used to be and where she had come from.

And, her brain reminded her, she still needed a spoon to cook her high on.

As the drugs cooked down into a magical cocktail, she pulled a sealed syringe from her pocket; it was her last one. She had already applied the rubber tube to her bicep.

The shelters and hospitals, unable to stem the flood of addicts, had decided if they couldn't stop them, at least they could help them stay as safe as they could. Nurses and doctors handed out needles and information to everyone who would listen.

She flicked off the lighter's flame from under the spoon and dropped it to the floor. The spoon was lowered more gently, careful not to spill a single drop. She opened the wrapper and pulled the syringe out, discarding the package without a thought.

Carefully she took off the protective sleeve and let the sharp needle tip Rest for a moment in the dark brown soup.

She pulled the plunger, filling the container.

The need was pulling at her now, playing her nerves like guitar strings as she angled the needle at the crook of her arm.

Now, she thought, *now, and I'll be able to leave my life behind for a little while.* A place where people didn't stare, or laugh. A place where she could fly.

She tapped her arm with two fingers, the line under her skin standing proud, the needle going into the offered vein. The sharp pain was something she would never get used to, but she fought through and pushed the heroin into her system. She felt the first rush of warmth, the first tingle of oblivion, and she welcomed it.

Reaching up with a hand that was starting to lose feeling, she tugged at the end of the tube, pulling it from her arm. The drug, free from the tight restriction, coursed through her body with the speed of quicksilver…and she fell to the mattress under her, a dreamlike smile on her face.

Alice's eyes opened and she sat up. Her body told her something was wrong; her highs had never ended like this.

She didn't feel confused, as she often did when she first surfaced… her mind was clear—her thoughts, too.

Frowning, she stood up. Her joints; knees, elbows and hips felt great, better than they had in years, her limbs didn't ache like they always did.

The only thing she could tell was wrong was the world around her. Everything was gloomy, like a picture seen through a slightly distorted camera lens.

She made her way towards the door…not knowing what was there, but curious anyway.

She poked her head into the hall and stared wide-eyed in both directions.

The hall on the other side seemed to go on forever, but the aspects were different. In one direction, it got smaller and smaller as it went, while the other grew bigger and bigger. Startled, she stood there, staring in wonder.

"Hello? H…hello? Is there anybody there?"

Her voice, whispering and afraid, echoed back to her in the still air.

She realized she couldn't just stand there…she had to find someone and ask what was going on.

On shaking legs, she walked towards the closest doorway and peered inside.

They?...He? sat in a plain wooden chair. She couldn't be sure if they were two people or just the one.

A huge obese body was squashed into the seat, the wooden arms bowing from the pressure. Two thin, wasted arms stuck out from the body, seemingly use-less.

It had four legs, but two were twig-like stumps of flesh, the skin black and coarse like aged leather.

Dee and his brother Dom stared at her from one face that contained the both of them.

It looked like the work of some mad sculptor,

their features melding together, constantly forming and reforming like melting candle wax.

The mouth opened, closed again…ran down the front of his/their face and disappeared into the flesh.

A hole opened instead, ragged and raw, the nubs of teeth seen in the dark cavity. A noise came from somewhere deep in its throat; a wet gurgle full of phlegm. It reached out with the stuck arms, the fingers of the hands opening and closing.

Alice backed out of the room and turned to run, her muscles already prepared.

"Well…hello there, beautiful."

Leroy stood in front of her, the huge toothy grin plastered across his face. The canines were long and sharp, more like a cat than a person. He reached up and plucked the glasses from his face. The skin where they touched his face stretched like taffy. And it was then she saw what was hidden behind the lenses.

She screamed; the image of the raw, weeping holes where his eyes used to be were forever stamped on her brain.

She ran, her feet pumping like pistons.

She ran down the hallway heading for a far end that receded further with every step she took. She looked over her shoulder, saw the black doorman, Leroy, striding after her. She was not going to get away… he would catch her.

She chose a door at random and ducked through. Her foot caught a step, and she tumbled down half a dozen risers before she could stop herself. Alice wrapped herself around the railing and looked down into the lobby below.

The floor was full of motion: figures crawling over each other. From where she stood, she made out one in particular; a man, his body wasted almost to a skin-covered skeleton. He held a syringe in one hand, the thin fingers clamped around it like a knife. He brought it down into his arm…missed the vein. He tried again, but missed for a second time. He opened his hand and dropped the needle, a thin-bladed knife appearing there instead. He stuck the point in the crook of one elbow and pulled the blade down to the wrist, opening the flesh like the petals of a flower.

Dropping the knife, he reached in and grabbed a flat vein with his fingers. Blood started to flow from the wound covering his arm, then the bodies of others around him. He grabbed the needle again and slid it into the fat worm-like strand, depositing the contents into his body.

Alice watched as the artery started to throb, then pulse with the beating of the man's heart. His head tilted back, a look of euphoria across his features. Back it went, back and back, the tendons in the neck stretching with the effort of the movement. The back of his head touched his back before the spine cracked with a sound like a gunshot.

The smile never left his face.

Another sat with his legs apart. He reached down and gently moved his testicles aside. He scraped at the fresh, scabbed-over tissue with the tip of a needle. Finding the almost flat vein, he plunged the hollow steel needle deep into his groin. He depressed the plunger and the look on his face was pure nirvana.

She saw others in the throes of ecstasy, individuals lost in the highs only the drugs could give them.

She walked down the rest of the stairs, unable or unwilling to take her gaze from the writhing, contorted bodies as they came ever closer.

Stepping onto the floor, Alice put her feet between two bodies that had their hands inside each others' chests. She could see the fingers working under the skin, coating internal organs with powder; the white talc-like granules leaking from the rents in the flesh as they worked.

She looked up to see a waving shadow in Hatter's office, shadows weaving to and fro on the walls and ceiling inside the room.

She passed body after body until she stepped through the archway.

The dealer known only as 'Hatter' was attached to the wall, his back flayed open, his ribs bent and piercing the plaster behind him. Pseudopods of waving flesh waved around his body, each tipped with a hypodermic needle. They waved and swayed with an obscene life of their own, dipping down to the desk with its array of pharmaceuticals, greedily sucking up powder and pills, then turning and pumping them through the man's body. Veins as big as snakes undulated under the skin. His face was a patchwork of broken blood vessels just below the surface.

His head lifted, the hat he always wore jammed onto his head, tendrils of flesh from his scalp interwoven between the fabric.

His voice when he spoke was a whisper. "Al-lissssss…"

She could only stand there and stare at the monstrosity, watching every part of him in constant motion.

She heard movement behind her and moved to one side. Figures started to file through the doorway, first as singles, then as groups.

They each carried the marks of their addiction; track marks on arms and legs, even some on the torso itself. They advanced on the thing wearing a man's face and drew the cocktail of drugs that flowed through him into themselves; the needle-tipped tentacles dispensing instead of taking.

Alice was scared for a minute or two, but the looks on the faces of the others made up her mind. She stepped forward to take her turn.

—

Leroy stood in the doorway and gestured at the body on the floor.

"Ahh crap. She was a good customer, too."

He reached down and gently moved a lock of hair from the woman's face. She had died with a smile, as if in possession of a secret. He saw the empty bags on the floor, the lighter and an antique silver spoon. He picked it up and put it in his pocket.

Hatter stood and looked at the black man. "Stick her in the alleyway. She'll be just another OD."

He turned and walked back into the decrepit hotel. The dead body all but forgotten already.

He lifted an old pocket watch from his coat, checking the time.

My name is Andy Holberry.
I herald from an island that no-one has heard of just
south of one of the busiest shipping lanes in the world.
I love to write and read...a lot.
Favourite authors are Guy Smith, James Herbert
and Stephen King. If some people are to be believed,
I am part robot, and I'm good with that lol

THE SIREN'S CURSE

Carietta Dorsch

Alaine's voice echoed through the ocean, a melody that seemed to capture the very essence of the sea, whispering like the waves and ocean breeze.

He sang of longing, and he cried out for love, of freedom and of acceptance, his voice a beacon calling out to those who dwelled on land. Alaine was trapped in a body that didn't align with his heart. He felt like a prisoner in his own skin, forced to live a life that wasn't his own. And so he sang, pouring all his pain and longing into his song, hoping someone would hear him and set him free.

Alaine climbed off the boulder, warm sea water dripping from his breasts, and tears in his eyes as he prepared himself to live under the sea as the King's daughter once again. Only on the boulder, only while he sang, was he ever truly free.

As he swam deeper into the depths, a large crack of laughter broke through to him.

What was that?

"*You,*" called out a woman's voice. "*I know what you seek.*"

"Me?" Alaine seemed to ask no one, for he couldn't see anyone.

Suddenly, she appeared.

She was a grotesque and repulsive creature. Alaine nearly yelled out in shock as he looked at her in horror. Her skin was a sickly color, like the belly of a rotting jellyfish, and it sagged and dripped from her bones like melted wax. Each bone was visible like a flesh-covered xylophone. Her eyes were two radiant orange balls, like embers from a fire that had long gone out from the beach parties Alaine watched sometimes. Her hair was a tangled mess of slimy locks, like a nest of sea snakes, and it seemed to writhe and twist behind her with a mind of their own.

"*I know what you seek*," she said again as her lip-less slit of a mouth turned upward. "*You seek freedom, Alaine.*" She smiled. Her voice was a husky croak, like the sound of the wind being strangled.

"How do you know my name?" Alaine asked as chills of discomfort spread over his body.

Her body was a mass of bulging, pulsing flesh, like a sack of writhing worms, and as she answered, it seemed to pulsate with each vowel. "*I know all, Alaine. And most of all, I know you.*"

"What do you mean?"

"*I know you are trapped,*" she whispered in his ear. "*You are trapped in a body that isn't yours.*"

"I'm not sure I understand."

"*I can give you what you desire,*" she seemed to taunt. "*I can give you what you seek. All you must do is ask.*"

"Please," he almost begged. "Please. I'd give anything."

"*Anything?*"

"Yes."

"*Then say you want it, and it will be.*"

"I want it," Alaine whispered to the empty ocean.

"*With true love comes only death and destruction,*" the sea creature whispered, the tone of the words seeming to make the very water colder and darker.

He turned around to see no one was near, no fish, no other mermaids, and even the distant sound of whales was too far to have been the voice he heard. He was alone, but again, he was used to that.

He knew it was time to go to his father's court meeting, to be the King's treasured daughter, but he just couldn't stomach it right now and needed to breathe fresh air, to feel human, to feel alive. He was so tired of feeling like a washed-up whale on a beach, dead inside and swelling with inner self-hate.

He swam through the water, his tail gliding effortlessly through the cool depths. He tried to escape his thoughts, the weight of the world pressing down on him. All he wanted was to be free, to escape the constant noise and chaos surrounding him.

As he swam further and further away from where he knew was a house but not a home, the water grew darker and colder. The only sound was the gentle lapping of the waves against the rocks above the surface. He felt a sense of peace wash over him, a temporary relief from the turmoil in his mind.

Finally, he reached a boulder sticking out underneath a cliff and touching sand. He rested his weary body against it, feeling the rough texture of the rock against his skin. He closed his eyes and let out a deep sigh, letting the water wash away his worries.

In that moment, he felt a sense of clarity wash over him.

Then, suddenly, he felt pain.

His scales started to crack open. As the scales fell away, his tail began to split. The green slime dripped and oozed from beneath the lifting scales and continued to seep from his pores as they fell to the sand, leaving a trail of foul-smelling sludge in their wake.

The sound of laughter from underneath the water

filled his eyes as he screamed in agony. Alaine let out a guttural cry as the scales continued to fall away, revealing a pale, human-like skin underneath. His tail, once strong and sleek, began to divide and elongate, forming legs that resembled those of a human man.

The green slime dripped, oozed and flowed from beneath the lifting scales, continuing to seep from his pores as they fell into the water.

Each scale that fell away felt like a dagger piercing his flesh. The foul-smelling sludge that trailed behind him left a sickening stench in the air.

Alaine stumbled forward, grasping the boulder with every ounce of energy he carried within himself, his new legs feeling weak and unsteady beneath him. He collapsed onto the sand, gasping for breath as he tried to make sense of what was happening to him.

It was her, he thought, *it was my wish from that sea creature.*

As the last of his scales fell away, Alaine looked down at his hands, now human in appearance. Tears welled up in his eyes as he realized that he was no longer the woman he had never been. He was something new, something different. He was finally the man he knew he was.

Alaine climbed onto the boulder, stood up on his shaky legs, and took his first steps as a human man. The water shifted beneath his feet, the waves crashed against it with gentle motion, and the ocean sky twinkled underneath the sky. And as he took his first step onto the sand, leaving his old life behind, Alaine knew that he was ready for whatever lay ahead.

Even though he was the happiest he had ever been, he couldn't shake the laughter he had heard when his scales began to fall out.

The laughter was quickly forgotten, and once again his heart filled with overpowering bliss. He couldn't resist the urge to sing out with joy. And so he sang, a beautiful melody that spoke of freedom and comfort.

*

Prince James was the first to hear Alaine's song. He was a brooding and troubled man, haunted by his past and searching for something to fill the void within him. Alaine's song spoke directly to his heart, and he was helpless to resist. He needed to know where the song was coming from.

The song gave him hope, it made him feel as if all was going to be okay, even though his family would disown him if they knew he didn't want to marry the princess they had in mind. No, he wanted not her, nor any woman for that matter—for he wanted a handsome prince by his side. In fact he longed to find a man who saw him for himself, instead of a royal family member.

He walked with determination and a heart full

of hope as the song grew louder. His feet sank into the sand with a gentle resistance, as if making him work for each step. For each step made him feel the pull toward the song even more, bringing him another step closer to the prize.

His eyes fell on Alaine. The Prince watched as he danced and twirled on the shore, stark naked and unashamed. Tracing the ripples in his abs and watching the water beads fall down his body caused Prince James to bite his lips and moan with fantasy, and their promises of making them become reality.

Alaine stopped in his dance as his eyes finally gravitated toward Prince James.

He's the most beautiful man I have ever seen, Alaine thought.

He's the most beautiful man I have ever seen, Prince James thought.

They seemed to step toward each other on the same step, their stride matching each other, both smiling with twinkling eyes of wonder and disbelief.

Arms as open as their hearts they finally touched and embraced each other. No words were exchanged, just a smile and a warm, welcoming kiss. Nothing else was needed or desired; they had both found what they were missing from themselves.

Vulnerability seized them both as they embraced each other with careless wonder. Their lips finding the other's, as if they knew all along it was this very person that they were searching for.

But then, suddenly, a scream broke the loving moment into shatters. Prince James let out a blood-curdling scream of pain as Alaine involuntarily ripped most of Prince James' tongue from his mouth. Alaine was shocked and disturbed by his actions, yet somehow he understood this was the price the sea creature spoke of. He found his body, but he will never find love.

In a sudden, violent motion, he ripped the remaining piece of Prince James' tongue out of his mouth, tearing a part of his throat and mouth in the process. Blood gushed from the torn flaps of meat that now dangled from his mouth, staining his clothes and painting the sand a deep burgundy.

Prince James let out a guttural scream of pain and shock, his eyes wide with horror as he tried to comprehend what had just happened. Alaine stood before him, sadness on his face as he held the severed tongue in between his lips, the blood dripping down his neck and flowing down his torso.

As James lay on the ground, clutching his bleeding throat, Alaine screamed out in horror and in disappointment.

How could I have been so stupid? he thought.

Without hesitation, Alaine clawed at his own throat and ripped out his own jugular. As the blood cascaded in a downpour, he laid next to Prince James and held his dying frame as gently as he could. As gently as the soft touch of Death himself, he placed one final kiss on Prince James' lips.

*

Love, the eternal tease. A sensual siren's call that beckons us with promises of pleasure, passion, and belonging. We crave the touch, the taste, the scent of another's skin, the soft whispers in the dark, the gentle caress that sets our souls aflame with hidden passion and forbidden pleasures.

But, alas, love is a cruel mistress. She tantalizes us with glimpses of ecstasy, only to leave us shrouded in the mist of heartache and the anguish, never having found its elusive promise. We grasp, we cling, we fight to find something to hold on to with all our energy and strength, yet our fingers only graze fleeting moments of bliss, but like rice in our hands falling from between our fingers, they slip away, leaving us with only the ache of longing and the painful sensation of rejection.

And yet, we cannot help but be drawn back, like moths to the flame, helpless to resist the allure of connection, of flesh, of pleasure. For in the depths of another's embrace, we find a fleeting sense of belonging, of reunion of self-acceptance, of transcendence to the very limits of our heart's capabilities of feeling something good about ourselves.

But, as it is with Alaine's longing and the sea creature's promise of freedom from the chains of this longing, love is a game of power, a delicate waltz of desire and ballet of control. We will always crave connection. We will always long to be consumed by passion, but we dread being devoured by the violent heat of lust. We will always want to lose ourselves, but we're terrified of getting lost and never finding ourselves or another to understand us.

In the end, love, just as self-acceptance, is a sensual illusion, a fleeting fantasy that vanishes within seconds of thinking you have it. We're only left with the bitter taste of longing, and the ache of unfulfilled desire forever. Our tongue will only know the taste of true freedom yet our throats will never know the sensation of swallowing that freedom. For it evaporates too quickly and leaves our hearts empty and eternally hungry.

This is the Siren's curse.

There is no escaping it.

It curses everyone.

Including you.

Carietta Dorsch has loved horror movies since she was a little girl watching them at a way too earlier age and loves even more to share her love of horror with her writing. She also writes poetry, romance, and true crime.

THE TOYMAKER

DEVIN CABRERA

Onlookers gasped as they saw the silhouette of a man on a curtain being stabbed through the heart by a knight on his noble steed. The man collapsed to his knees, clutching at his chest with both hands before falling to the floor and letting out an anguished moan as he died. The crowd of people, if you could call four people in the castle square a crowd, clapped as the shadow of the knight bowed from his horse. The light behind the curtain was extinguished, and the shadows disappeared as the Toymaker walked out of his booth. In his hands, he carried two marionette puppets. They were made of wood, with pieces of string running through their joints at one end and connecting to a cross piece in the Toymaker's hands.

The Toymaker walked in front of the crowd, eyeing up his audience. When he was sure he had their full attention, his foot caught a rock he had placed in front of his booth. Instantly, it appeared like he had stumbled, and the marionettes fell out of his hands, tumbling toward the ground.

Another gasp rang out from one of the boys in the crowd as he imagined the puppets getting smashed to pieces on the ground.

At the very last moment, before they could hit the ground, the puppet's strings snapped taut, splaying out all of their limbs, and they began to dance an inch above the soil. The Toymaker moved his hands back and forth, and the marionettes moved with him, bending and walking like no lifeless object should be able to.

This was what the Toymaker did.

He built all his toys by hand by candlelight, and

by day, he would make them dance and sing to the delight of any onlookers who walked by. Occasionally, they would throw him a coin or two for his troubles. Other times, the Toymaker would make nothing, meaning he would have to go home hungry that night. It pushed him to try harder each day and to create a rotation of new characters and stories to keep the crowds coming back day after day.

The Toymaker enjoyed what he did, and the show he was working on at present was going splendidly. He would probably go home with enough money by the end of the day to buy himself a loaf of bread and some soup to go with it.

These were the thoughts running through his mind when Sir Henry walked by.

Sir Henry was one of the King's knights and just about the meanest man inside the castle's walls. He just so happened to come upon the Toymaker's booth while the man was putting on a skit about a commoner making a fool out of a knight who looked very similar to a depiction of Sir Henry himself.

"What the hell is going on here?" Sir Henry asked.

The crowd scattered; they knew whatever was coming next wouldn't be good, and they didn't want to be on the receiving end of Sir Henry's anger. They had seen it before, and it typically didn't end well for the other person.

Sir Henry ripped the knight marionette out of the Toymaker's grasp, brought it to his face, and inspected it.

"Do you think this is funny?" Sir Henry asked, turning to face the crowd, then back to the Toymaker. "Well? Do you?"

"This particular show is meant to make people

laugh, yes," the Toymaker said.

Sir Henry grimaced and squeezed the marionette until the wood splintered in his grasp.

"Hey! You can't do that!" the Toymaker shouted, moving to stop the man, but Sir Henry shoved the man into the mud.

The knight ripped down the curtains of the Toymaker's booth, revealing everything inside. He tossed all the other toys to the ground as hard as he could, then spit at the feet of the puppeteer. Sir Henry jumped back onto his horse, preparing to disembark, but then decided he wasn't quite done yet.

He turned the horse around, forcing it to stomp on all the man's toys, crushing them beneath its weight. Then he dug his heels into the horse's backside, and it pitched forward, bucking its hind legs backward and knocking over the lantern that the Toymaker had used for his shadow puppets.

The flame was still lit, and as it hit the ground, the oil inside it spread around the booth, setting everything ablaze in an instant.

Sir Henry laughed, then rode off on his horse.

There was nothing the Toymaker could do.

What had started out as a good day had turned into a disaster. His life's work was ruined. He was finished. His booth and all of his toys, which were made of dry wood and hay, were turned to ash in a matter of minutes.

With tears falling down his face, the Toymaker grabbed what coins he had left, then walked out of the castle, beginning the long trek to his shack.

On the long walk home, he had a lot of time to think, and by the time he closed the door behind him, he knew what must be done.

The Toymaker opened the door to his closet and

reached his hand into the back of a shelf at the top. He reached farther and farther back into the shadows where everything was hidden.

When he finally pulled his arms back, he carried with him a chest that had been passed down from Toymaker to Toymaker.

He placed the chest on the ground and carefully undid each leather strap holding it shut. When the final strap was loosened, he swung the lid open, spraying dust into the air and allowing the sun's rays to illuminate the face of the puppet inside.

The Toymaker whispered in the puppet's ear, and a moment later, its eyes fluttered open.

They were black as night and filled with anger. The puppet had one purpose, one job it was meant to carry out. Generation after generation, it would be called upon for revenge.

The Toymaker picked the puppet up, set it on the windowsill next to the open window, and then turned around to close the chest.

When he looked back, the puppet was gone.

That night, Sir Henry woke up gasping for air.

He had had a dream that he had been thrown from his horse, and the wind had been knocked out of him. The man looked around his room, thankful it was all in his head. He was safe in his chambers; nothing could touch him here.

Nothing but the puppet in the corner of the room, its dark eyes blending in with the shadows that hid it.

Sir Henry jumped as he heard a sound like two pieces of a wooden wind chime knocking together.

The room was dark, with only the light of the

moon streaming.

Sir Henry rubbed at his eyes, willing them to adjust to the darkness quicker as he scanned the room. He could feel his heart beating rapidly in his chest, and sweat dripped down his brow as he looked back and forth across the area.

The sound came again, this time from the other side of the room.

Whatever it was, it was moving.

Sir Henry tossed the blankets off. He was hesitant initially, but after taking a deep breath, he placed his feet on the cold stone floor.

If he could just get to the hallway, he could grab one of the torches on the wall and use it to see the intruder. Then, he would be able to fight the person like a man.

Taking another breath, Sir Henry got to his feet

and began to run across the room toward the door.

His bare feet slapped against the stone floor with every step, and he was eerily aware of the sounds his steps made as he ran.

He was also aware of the other set of steps, which were growing louder and louder as they followed him to the door.

Sir Henry picked up the pace, not bothering to stop. A moment later, he hit the door, knocking it open with his shoulder and hearing a crack. He grabbed his right shoulder, knowing that it was probably dislocated, but he kept going.

He reached for the burning torch hung on the wall outside his door and ripped it from its socket.

Sir Henry shoved the torch back the way he had come, toward the person following him.

But no one was there.

Sir Henry breathed heavily. He wasn't built to run; that's what his horse was for.

He looked down the hall toward safety. He could go that way, but how could he tell someone that he was scared, that there was an intruder in his room that had frightened Sir Henry himself?

There was no way he could look anyone in the eye after that. No, he had to handle this on his own.

Sir Henry took a few steps back into the room, his torch held out in front of him with his left arm and his right arm hanging limply at his side. Once he was fully into the room, he swung the torch to the left, seeing nothing in that corner.

He spun around, looking in a different direction, but couldn't make out anything there either.

A breeze wafted in through the open window, causing the torch flames to jump and the shadows in the room to grow large and menacing.

None of this made things any easier on Sir Henry, who shone his light toward every shadow, slowly backing up until his back was against the windowsill.

He heard a noise behind him and turned to see a vulture floating with the breeze outside his window.

Sir Henry gulped.

Vultures tended to fly in areas where death was near. They weren't a good sign.

Just then, Sir Henry felt a tap on his ankle.

He spun around as fast as he could, making him drop the torch on the ground.

Standing in front of it, the puppet seemed to grow larger, its shadow covering Sir Henry's entire body.

Sir Henry screamed and fell to the ground. Only then did he realize that the tap on his ankle wasn't a tap at all.

The puppet had taken one of its strings, which were apparently made out of thin razor wire, and wrapped it around his ankle before pulling it taught, severing his foot from the rest of his leg.

His foot was still planted in front of the window where he had left it.

Sir Henry tried to scream once more, hoping that someone would hear him and come to his rescue, but before he could do so, he felt a pain in his throat.

He opened his eyes to see the puppet standing over him, its wooden hands dancing in front of his face. He felt entranced by the puppet's dark eyes and found himself getting lost in them, losing all feeling in his body as he did so.

Meanwhile, the puppet was sawing at the man's throat with its razor wire, creating a second mouth where his neck should be.

The man tried to speak but only managed to blow bubbles in the dark blood that poured out of his throat.

Sir Henry's vision was going dark as he was rapidly losing blood, but he was alive long enough to see the puppet stab him in each of his joints before everything went black.

A second vulture joined the first and would soon be followed by a third and a fourth. They floated on the breeze, inhaling the scent of fresh blood as they waited for the puppet to finish its work.

They would be rewarded for their patience.

When the sun rose the next morning, it cast a shadow on the tower next to Sir Henry's.

The shadow was of a knight. A knight that hung from strings tied to his window.

Each of the strings ran through one of Sir Henry's joints, and he was bleeding from his knees and elbows.

As the castle awoke, a little boy felt a drop of liquid on his head as he walked nearby.

He reached his hand up, smearing blood across his forehead. The boy looked to the sky and screamed.

It drew the attention of a crowd, who all paused to stare at the man, his body convulsing on the strings like a marionette dancing in the breeze.

The Toymaker stirred in his sleep as the sun rose over the nearby hill. As his eyes adjusted to the light, he found the puppet sitting where he had left it on his windowsill.

Devin Cabrera develop age, devouring books at every turn. As an adult, this love of stories turned into a career, working on both the big and small screen, bringing characters to life and captivating audiences. With a diverse range of projects under his belt, from gripping dramas  such as Pretty Little Liars to thrilling reality shows like Deadliest Catch, he has proven himself as an excellent storyteller in all its forms.

But it wasn't until recently that he decided to turn his talents to the page. Sitting down at his desk, he painstakingly crafted a story, honing every word until it was just right. With a fresh perspective and a lifetime of experience with stories, he promises to take readers on a journey they won't soon forget.

PLAGUE BRINGER:
A DARK FAIRYTALE

L.W. Young

Once upon a time, a lowly thief named Caleb was sitting alone in his dank prison cell. He paid little mind to the miserable wails of the sick prisoners around him, knowing that someone would come by to let him out soon. Luck, after all, was his specialty.

The first to arrive was the guard, who suddenly fell into a coughing fit before dying on the floor in front of him. The second visitor came the next day, a stray hound whom Caleb attempted to coax to his aid, but the animal ran off after finding nothing but rotting remains to feed on. The day after, a third visitor came by: an unkempt little girl with fair, greasy hair who held a grubby teddy bear under her arm.

"Open my cell, little girl," Caleb cooed, not caring why she was here. "You'll do well to travel with me, as I'm the luckiest thief in all the land."

*Illustrations by Author L.W. Young

Clutching her bear, the girl seemed hesitant, but soon saw how Caleb was somehow unaffected by the deadly plague. She picked up the guard's keys and let him out of his cage, trailing behind him as they walked over the wart-ridden corpses piled up in the prison's gangways.

Reaching the exit, Caleb saw the stationed guards had been brutally murdered, with their remains dashed against the brick walls. The portcullis over the drawbridge had also been torn open as if made of tin, allowing Caleb to leave the dungeon. Caleb skipped merrily through the opened way, quite certain that he would not run into whatever beast had done this. The girl followed at his side as they walked into the fog.

The thick air seemed to glow with a toxic green hue all around them. Caleb whistled as he walked, playing with his pocket knife. The girl, meanwhile, shuffled alongside with her eyes to the ground, clutching her bear tightly.

On their travels, they reached an ancient oak tree ornamented with emerald leaves and plump acorns. On the trunk of the tree was a tiny door, barely big enough for a mouse to fit through. Caleb drew his knife and approached it, telling the girl to stay behind. As Caleb got closer, the door grew larger and larger until it was a suitable size for him to enter. It was only when he turned around that he realized that he had become smaller.

"Come in!" a keen voice coaxed through the half-open door. "We've been expecting you."

Opening the door, Caleb saw a gathering of naked pixie-like creatures with glowing skin and butterfly wings, buzzing around the hollow of the tree trunk. They giggled as they saw him.

"Expecting me?" Caleb asked as he walked inside.

"You must be exhausted," said a pixie, ignoring

his question. "Why not refresh yourself? We have plenty of food!"

The hovering pixies drew back, revealing a long dining table decorated with meat, wine, and puddings.

"All for me?" Caleb laughed, sitting himself down. "It's been a while since I've seen such a feast!"

"Of course," the second fairy gestured. "However, in exchange, we want the girl."

"The girl?" Caleb asked. "The one out there?"

The fairies nodded.

"Then I'll just fetch her," Caleb declared, rising to his feet. "Just let me take this ham leg and peach syrup to coax her."

"Please." The fairies licked their lips and rubbed their hands. "We'll be waiting!"

Their hungry eyes followed Caleb out of the tree-house. Caleb walked back to the girl, returning to his normal size. However, as the girl looked up at him sadly, Caleb found himself regretting his decision.

"I suppose you've been useful to me once," Caleb declared. "Perhaps you'll be useful again."

With that, Caleb turned on his heels and launched the glass beaker of sticky peach syrup at the small open door on the base of the tree trunk. The fairies, who had been gathering at the entrance, quickly found themselves swamped in sugary syrup, which weighed them down while flying shards of glass lacerated their tiny bodies.

As they struggled, birds and insects descended from up high to finish them off. The fairies' helpless screams were barely audible as Caleb and the girl carried on towards town.

Later, Caleb and the girl came to the mouth of a stone underpass. The girl seemed hesitant to go inside, but Caleb strode confidently onwards as he absently chewed the last of the meat from the ham leg, encouraging her to go with him. Suddenly, as they were walking through the dark, a pair of gleaming eyes lit up in front of them.

"Hello, good sir," a voice snarled from the shadows.

The girl dashed behind Caleb as a lantern illuminated the face of a grinning dog wearing a velvet top hat. The beast had a long, wet snout, was standing upright on its hind legs, and wore a purple coat adorned with many pockets.

"Who might you be, doggie?" Caleb responded with his mouth half full of food.

"I, good fellow, am the Top Hound. I am a merchant from far away," the creature replied, tipping his hat as his glowing eyes caught sight of the girl. "And HELLO especially to you, little one!"

The Top Hound crouched down to eye level with the girl, panting with its tongue lolling out of its mouth. The girl shrank away from its rotten breath.

"What do you want?" Caleb asked impatiently, holding his nose.

"Why, I'm in the business of selling gold, sir," the Top Hound replied, rising to its feet again. "All I ask in return is a square meal to satiate my hunger."

"I don't have anything," Caleb replied.

The Top Hound noted the empty bone in Caleb's hand before sizing the girl up with his saucer-plate eyes.

"Well, in absence of food, this little one's services might prove most… appetizing." The dog grinned, licking his chops.

"Okay, sure," Caleb shrugged, pushing the girl forward. "Sorry, little one."

The girl yelped tearfully as she was shoved into the Top Hound's care. Caleb felt a little bad, but he wasn't one to say no to gold. Caleb could not imagine a world where gold did not have at least *some* value.

"A wise choice, sir—a wise choice indeed." The Top Hound slobbered, rubbing its paws together. "Please, take this in exchange."

The Top Hound reached into one of its many pockets and pulled out a tiny cloth pouch, handing it to Caleb.

"What's this?" Caleb snorted, pulling apart the sack's drawstrings and poking the glittering dust inside. "This isn't gold!"

"Ah, but it is gold *dust*," the dog replied proudly, pointing his paw in Caleb's face. "When a fistful of this stuff is blown to the wind, it will grant its owner one magic wish."

"Rubbish!" Caleb cried. "You tricked me!"

"A deal's a deal." The creature tipped its hat. "Now, I shall take my leave…"

The girl tried to pull away as the Top Hound placed his paw on her back. However, Caleb was not one to be duped, and waved the clean ham bone in the Hound's face before it could turn away. The Top Hound, giving in to its animal nature, became transfixed by the rhythmic motion of the bone.

"Here, doggie," Caleb teased, waving the bone from side to side as the hound's pupils followed it like a metronome. "Fetch!"

With that, Caleb threw the bone into the depths of the tunnel behind him. The dog, dropping his lantern, collapsed onto all fours and went darting after it. This gave Caleb the chance to pick up the lantern for himself.

"Come on." He grabbed the girl's hand and pulled her along. "You'll forgive me, won't you?"

The girl was silent, which Caleb took for a yes.

Soon, the lantern's light was too far away for the Top Hound to see them. His lost, helpless howls followed the pair all the way down the tunnel until they finally emerged out of the underpass and into the evening twilight.

When the duo reached town, the cobblestone

sidewalks were littered with bodies, and a rancid stink clung to everything. The only sounds were the whistling wind and the rusty groan of the swinging pub signs. However, one place which Caleb hoped was still active was an old brothel he used to visit in his teens. To his delight, he found the place was still in business.

"Hey there, handsome." Caleb was greeted at the entrance by a slender young woman with round hips, rosy cheeks, and a curtain of blonde hair concealing half of her heavily-painted face. "I'm Rosetta. Looking for a good time tonight?"

"Sounds tempting," Caleb eyed her up and down. "However, I have no money."

"Oh, that's a pity," Rosetta pouted. "Tell you what, we'll simply take the girl as payment. I'm sure she'll make a useful house servant. Won't you, precious?"

Rosetta bent down to the little girl's level, folding her nightgown into her lap while pinching the girl's cheek in a motherly fashion. The girl retreated, snapping her teeth.

Caleb found it difficult to say no to such a beautiful face and allowed Rosetta to grab the girl's arm. The girl clung to his leg, screaming as Rosetta pulled her away. Caleb tried not to think about the girl's tearful screams as he spent the evening with Rosetta, helping himself to an opium pipe once he was fully spent.

Later that night, while Caleb was drugged and fast asleep, Rosetta and her friends used the opportunity to rob him. However, Caleb had little except his overcoat, pocketknife, and bag of useless gold dust.

"Worthless bastard!" Rosetta shrieked, throwing the pouch back at him. "Let's dump him on the edge of town somewhere!"

The next morning, Caleb found himself dumped in a ditch on the outskirts of town.

"What happened?" he moaned, feeling desperately sorry for himself as he clutched his throbbing head. "I thought I was supposed to be lucky."

Could it have been that it was the girl's presence protecting him this whole time rather than his own luck? With all that had happened, Caleb was starting to believe it, as otherwise he would not have been imprisoned in the first place.

That was when he noticed that the empty sack given to him by the Top Hound was still looped around his small toe and a trail of sparkling gold dust spilled from it, leading back into town. Caleb followed it, collecting as much dust as he could along the way. The effort took him until nightfall.

Back in town, Caleb spotted Rosetta sitting by the window on the brothel's top floor, brushing her hair. Caleb sneaked into the brothel and tiptoed up to Rosetta's bedroom, making a dash for the lady's current client while he was fast asleep on the bed.

Upon hearing a sharp pop, Rosetta spun around on her chair and saw her current client, an elderly gentleman, lying limp on her bed with a reddening pillow shoved on his face, now sporting a smoking bullet hole. Caleb was kneeling over the body and pointing the pistol he had snatched from the nightstand. Rosetta shrieked.

"Shut up!" Caleb demanded, cocking the hammer. "Tell me where the girl is, and I might let you live."

"I… I sold her to some priests who were offering good money for her. They even placed a blessing on this building." Rosetta pleaded with her arms up. "Please, don't hurt me!"

"I won't hurt you," Caleb sneered, relishing the sight of her body, "In fact, I have something better in mind…"

Holding her at gunpoint, Caleb emptied a chest lying at the foot of the bed and used the clothes to tie her up. In seconds, Rosetta was gagged and blind-folded, with her wrists and ankles knotted tightly to-gether like a trussed pig. Rosetta struggled against her restraints while pleading with Caleb, but her muffled screams were barely audible as he dragged her over to the empty clothes chest.

"Sorry, can't hear you," Caleb laughed, picking Rosetta up and stuffing her inside the chest. "Besides, I think I prefer you like this anyway."

Then, he slammed the lid shut and locked it from the outside. With Rosetta's dampened screams barely bothering him as he sat on the chest, Caleb pondered his next move. With little left, he pulled out the faint traces of gold dust he'd collected from his pocket.

"I hope this works." He cleared his throat. "Take me to wherever the girl is!"

Then, he blew the gold dust into the wind.

Suddenly, Caleb was transported to a dark chapel which hummed with low chanting. The hooded figures of dark-robed priests wandered about the place, their long shadows flickering along the candle-lit floor. Strapped to the altar in the centre of the room was the girl, struggling against her restraints as the lead priest approached her with a ceremonial dagger.

"Leave her alone!" Caleb stepped forward, brandishing his pocket knife. "She's just a child!"

"She is no mere child, but an agent of darkness," said the priest, turning. "She was sent by demons to spread disease across this world."

"W…what are you talking about?" Caleb faltered, lowering his weapon.

The priest removed her hood and revealed a withered, pale-faced old woman with wispy white hair and sunken dark eyes.

"This child was born in sin under the moon of a blood-red eclipse, and her unholy presence brings the plague across this land," the dark priest appealed tiredly. "By ending her life in this holy blood ritual, we can end all of our suffering."

The girl screamed at the priests, pulling harder against her restraints, and trying to reach for her teddy, which lay discarded by the side of the altar.

"At least let her have her bear!" Caleb started forward, kneeling for the stuffed animal.

"NO!"

The dark priest tried to stop him, but Caleb had already stepped over the row of candles and passed the teddy bear to where the girl lay strapped on the altar. As her tiny hands grabbed it, the girl's eyes lit up with a blood red glow and she began whispering words that Caleb didn't understand into the bear's ear.

"Do you realize what you have just done?" The priest turned to Caleb, stabbing a withered, accusing finger at him.

Caleb shrugged innocently. Then, in a shock-wave of energy that blew out the candles surrounding the altar, the mangy teddy twisted and contorted until it no longer resembled a teddy at all, but a hulking, demonic monster which towered over the altar and priests alike.

Inside the darkness, Caleb thought he could see a lion-like head, goat legs, and claws like great scythes on each of the beast's hands. The monster made a piercing roar that froze Caleb's soul. The priests made a dive for it, but the monster easily overpowered them, cleaving them in half with a swing of its arm, and knocking Caleb against a nearby pillar.

Caleb woke in darkness. The flickering embers from the candles, doused by the blood of the massacred priests, provided the only faint light. The silhouette of the newly freed girl stood before him, the bloodstained teddy now back in her grasp. Despite his fear, Caleb tried to smile at her.

"Y…you surely are a lucky one," Caleb panted breathlessly. "I'll do well to travel with you."

Caleb could tell she was smiling back at him.

"I suppose you've been useful to me once," she agreed. "Perhaps you'll be useful to me again."

Caleb accepted and took her hand, ignoring the fact that her voice bore the tone of a thousand swarming flies.

L.W. Young graduated from the University of Kent with a BA Honors degree in English literature and creative writing. He has experience with writing for theater, film and YouTube, and is a passionate advocate of mindfulness and raising awareness of mental health issues. His favourite authors and influences include an eclectic bag: ranging from Stephen King to Cormac McCarthy to Ray chandler to David Mitchell to Kazuyo Ishigoda to Margaret Atwood and Colson Whitehead. However, if you ask him, he would probably tell you his favourite books are the Point Horror novels he read in his High School library as a teenager.

GOLDIE AND THE WOLF
BILL FREAS

The embers smoldered diabolically over the residential wreckage as the sky's pre-dawn glow highlighted these remnants of a night of pure carnage. Twenty-four hours ago, two modest houses stood side by side here, their inhabitants the victims of a violent catastrophe.

Goldie ran away from home again. She was a troubled, blonde girl of seventeen who finally wrapped up her third stint in juvie, only to come home and stab her mother's abusive, deadbeat boyfriend with a rusty corkscrew. The puncture wound wasn't fatal, but the wrath of the creep and the long arm of the law weren't worth sticking around for.

Instead, she camped out meagerly in the north end of the woods, where those two modest houses sat quietly. The one on the left sent her into a deep obsession. It was the home of three bears – Papa, Mama, and Baby Bear. They were the family she always wanted, the one she desperately needed. She spent her days squatting in the brush, watching the bears live a happy life, and cutting her arms and legs with a cheap razor she lifted from the convenience store in town. The bears proved to her that a loving family was real. Sadly, though, they were not *her* family – not yet, at least.

Next door to the bears' house, three little pigs resided. They were brothers very close in age, each of them working together as building contractors. Theirs wasn't a fancy home, either. Made mostly of straw and sticks, the house had old-fashioned scaffolding in place while the brothers gradually converted the structure to brick, which would help them better endure the harsh forest winters. They worked on the home themselves as their time and budget allowed. Like the Bear family, they, too, were simple, hardworking folk.

Days and nights passed for months. Goldie remained in the woods, watching her dream family and ingesting the most extreme hallucinogenic mushrooms the forest had to offer. The girl was slowly losing her mind, and there was no help in sight for the runaway.

Her obsession soon brought sadness, and then anger. She was going to be a part of that family whether they knew it or not. One Saturday night came around, and the three bears had a honey banquet to go to in a neighboring village. Goldie knelt in the weeds and waited for the bears' Dodge Windstar minivan to coast out of the driveway and head off to their destination.

When the coast was clear, she tiptoed to the back

door of the house and examined the locks. She had a few tricks up her sleeve from her short stint of turning tricks in the big city. A thoughtful john once showed her how to pick locks, and the girl never forgot the tutorial. She was into the house as fast as the three bears were into their honey.

Goldie wandered through the small home and took in the sights of normal, stable family living. A tear ran down her cheek. It was an idyllic environment that she had never witnessed in person. Her dream had come true... almost. As she passed through the kitchen, she came upon three bowls of fresh, uneaten porridge – a yummy supper side dish that the bears didn't have time to get to this evening.

The girl was starving and still a bit stoned from forest mushrooms, so that porridge looked mighty enticing to her growling belly. She had never eaten good porridge in her entire life. Her drunk mother unlawfully used up most of their weekly welfare money on cigarettes and booze, and she only bought the lousy, cheap porridge box mix from the dollar store. It was typically stale and had a noticeable scattering of rat feces among its grains.

Goldie was mildly curious about why the bears didn't eat their porridge, but it didn't matter to her for very long. She grabbed a spoon and sat down in Papa's chair – too big and hard. She slid over to Mama's chair – far too soft and wobbly. Baby's chair was just right – comfy yet sturdy.

She decided to try Baby's porridge first, as well. It was perfect. She gobbled it down so quickly that she nearly choked. As the warm, delicious grains hit her aching, empty stomach, she disappeared into a peaceful trance. Her state of bliss soon led her to digest her hearty porridge dinner, in the cozy, snug confines of Baby's bed, which was also just right for her.

Letting her guard down and relaxing too deeply was a huge mistake. As she snored her little, blonde head off in bed, the hours passed, unbeknownst to the sleeping runaway. She awoke abruptly to the cool steel barrel of a .38 Special pressed into her cheek.

"Move an inch and you'll be doing the headless limbo at your own funeral," the gun's handler said with a stern voice. It was Papa Bear, and he was pissed.

Goldie's eyes widened with fear, and her heart pounded through her brain. Her vacation was over, and her dream family was not so welcoming.

"Papa, why is this broad in my bed?" Baby asked, annoyed.

"Stay back, son," said Papa. "She could be dangerous. Girls like this usually carry drugs, weapons, and plenty of venereal diseases."

Goldie carefully spoke up. "Look... I'm really

sorry. I just... needed some food."

"How'd you get in here?" Papa questioned.

Mama chimed in. "I told you we should've changed the locks and gotten one of those security systems."

"You're the one in the woods, right?" Papa asked Goldie, who stayed silent. "You think I'm blind, bitch? I know everything that happens in those woods. I've seen you out there, you dirty, lazy tramp."

Mama continued complaining. "To think that she could've seen the basement. All that hard work we put in, and it would've been down the drain."

"I never saw the basement. I just had some porridge and took a nap. That's it. I only wanted to... be a part of a family," Goldie confessed.

Papa replied, "You don't deserve a family, you worthless slag. You're a no-good piece of street trash, a blight on society. You're lower than the festering mold growing on the rotten logs out in those woods. You're less than nothing."

Tears welled up in Goldie's eyes. Things here were no different than what she was used to back home.

"Well, what are we going to do with this runaway street bum, Papa?" Mama asked.

Papa thought for a second, a malevolent look forming in his eyes. "The basement could always use another... piece of furniture."

Suddenly, some loud chatter from next door drew all of their attention away and broke the suspense. The bears looked up and listened as one of the three little pig brothers was engaged in a heated argument with someone on the front porch of his house.

This distraction provided the perfect opportunity for Goldie. She wasted no time, kneeing Papa in the groin before swatting his gun away. The big bear shrieked in pain and toppled to the floor. The girl then charged at Mama and slammed her into the wall. Baby approached and took a wild swing at Goldie, but he missed as the girl sprinted out the back door and scurried away into the woods.

The frightened runaway ducked into some thick brush and caught her breath, recovering from the terrifying encounter. The quarrel at the pigs' house was now close enough for her to see and hear. She watched closely while the pig brother continued exchanging vitriolic words with a rugged, stocky wolf dressed like a rogue member of a nasty biker gang.

"I'm not your fall guy anymore, Randy! You owe me!" the wolf shouted.

"I don't owe you shit! We're square, remember?" the pig replied.

"I do six years hard time for you, and you say

we're square?"

"If you don't get off my property right now, I'm calling the cops about a psychotic, trespassing stalker ex-con who won't leave me and my brothers alone! Now, beat it, you crazy asshole!" the pig yelled before slamming the front door aggressively in the wolf's face.

Goldie watched closely as the wolf stormed off in a huff. Carefully, she followed him through the woods until he found a spot to settle down and start a campfire. He, too, was a lonely, destitute soul, a forgotten ghost of the forest. The wolf stared into the mesmerizing flames of his campfire, his mind wandering off to dark places.

"I'm thinking we could help each other out," Goldie said. Her voice came out of nowhere and startled the wolf.

He instantly snapped to attention and went on the defensive. "Who the hell are you? Did you follow me? Did the pigs send you?"

The girl waltzed casually toward the fire. "The bears have something I want, and it sure sounds like the pigs have something you want."

"I used to supervise building projects for them, those bastards," he explained. "They were cooking the books, and guess who took the fall for it? Promised me a payoff when I got out of the clink. Still waiting. What's your story? What is it you're after?"

Goldie answered, "Well, I wanted something there that it seems I can never have. So, I'm taking the next best thing. Apparently, they've got shit in the basement, valuable shit. They were nervous that I might have seen it down there."

"Did you...see it?"

She smirked and shook her head flirtatiously before sauntering closer to him. It was clear she was a pro, too young to know how to pull off this act this well. The girl sat down next to the wolf and ran her fingers seductively through his fur.

"What do you say, sexy? Partners in crime?" she asked.

He peered into her devious eyes, falling for her persuasion harder by the second. Finally, he nodded with reluctance.

"What's your name?" Goldie questioned.

"BB... BB Wolf – short for Big Bad Wolf," he replied.

"So, BB... Are you as big and bad as your name?"

He looked down, his thoughts and emotions pulling him in ten different directions.

"Here, have one," the girl said. She then fed him one of her hallucinogenic mushrooms.

"What is it?"

"Just a little snack... Loosen us up a bit," she answered before consuming a mushroom as well.

In less than a minute, both of them were tripping. Goldie saw purple horses darting across the night sky. The horses soon melted into a yellow starburst that danced around the moon and swirled into a blue wind. The colorful gust of air let out a psychedelic laugh that rang through the dense forest and made Goldie smile peacefully.

The wolf's trip, however, was not so pleasant. His hallucinations manifested nightmarish visions that sent him shrieking and howling in agony. Goldie backed away from him, unsettled by what was happening. With adrenaline pumping at abnormally high levels, the wolf growled. His sharp teeth dripped with saliva, and his eyes went bloodshot with severely dilated pupils.

The enraged beast glared at the girl and then

raced off, back in the direction of the two houses. Fighting her best judgment and giving in to her spiteful emotions, Goldie took advantage of her new friend's maniacal state and cautiously followed his tempestuous path.

The wolf marched up to about thirty feet in front of the little pigs' house and stood there defiantly. Still raging at incredible intensity, he let out an ungodly howl that shook both houses and the forest around them.

"Little pigs, little pigs! You owe me, so let me in!" he hollered.

The sounds of three shotguns pumping echoed lightly before the three pigs each leaned out of a window at the front of their house, bearing their weapons.

"Not by the hair-trigger on my Mossberg 12-gauge! Not a chance in hell, asshole!" the one pig replied.

"Then, I'll huff, and I'll puff, and I'll blow this shit box in!" the wolf threatened.

"Try us!" another pig said, gripping his shotgun confidently.

Goldie ran up to her hiding spot in the brush, just in time to observe the tense standoff. She wasn't the only one watching. Her eyes caught sight of Papa and Mama Bear peering curiously at the confrontation, from a side window of their home.

The wolf seized a massive breath and let it rip on the pigs' house. The colossal force of air knocked the pigs off-kilter and tore down the home's scaffolding, sticks, and hay. Structurally, a few unfinished brick walls and corner joints were all that were left standing after the wolf's strike.

"You want some more? Gimme what's mine!" the wolf shouted.

The pigs gathered themselves and remained resistant.

"Come and get some!" the one yelled.

A loud, forceful hissing noise crescendoed while the wolf gathered another attack breath. The pigs once again readied their shotguns and took aim. Goldie watched intensely as the face-off looked to reach its violent climax.

"Don't do it, scumbag!" one pig shouted.

The wolf refused to comply. Just as he let loose his next air assault, the pigs opened fire. The shotgun slugs barely had a chance to strike the wolf dead before the entire lot exploded into a massive fireball. The hissing noise was from a torn gas line blown open by the wolf's first big breath, and the sparks given off by the shotgun blasts were the ignition needed to send the pigs and what was left of their home, up in flames.

Always the ready opportunist, Goldie seized this disastrous moment to make her move. As Papa and Mama Bear gazed in utter shock at the fiery wreckage, the girl slipped through the back door of their house, just as she had done before. This time, she grabbed a steak knife from the butcher's block in the kitchen before sneaking into the dining room.

"The cops and fire department will be here in less than ten minutes, Mama. We have to pack some bags and hit the road. Get a move on," Papa Bear said to his wife.

They hustled away from the window and into the dining room, where they were met with an unexpected sight. Goldie stood there staring at them. Her one hand had a hard grip on Baby Bear, and her other hand held the steak knife firmly to his throat. There was momentary silence as the bear parents processed what was happening.

"All I wanted was to belong to something good, something special," said Goldie. "But now, I don't give a shit. I'm cashing out. So, we're going down to your precious basement, and I'm collecting my severance. Give me any trouble at all, and Junior here gets his jugular opened up all over your pristine, hand-knit area rugs."

The bears had no choice but to obey. Slowly, they led her down to the dark basement. A single lightbulb clicked on to reveal an empty and unfinished space – nothing but concrete. Goldie peered around, perplexed by the absence of much of anything.

"Are you fucking kidding me?" she asked.

"We're simple folk, young lady," Mama replied. "What did you expect?"

"Don't give me that shit," the girl said. "I woke up to your husband jamming a revolver into my face. Save the innocent routine, lady."

Papa interjected, "You mean when we found you trespassing in our home after breaking and entering?"

Goldie clammed up. She was stuck in a tricky predicament at this point.

"Mama, she won't go in the room, right?" Baby whispered.

Goldie suddenly perked up. "What room?"

"I'm not sure what you're talking—" Mama began to say.

The girl interrupted and got in Baby's face. "What room, kid?"

"Run, Baby, run, go!" Mama shouted.

Baby elbowed Goldie in the gut and started to spin around to escape, but the girl jerked her knife-bearing hand back reflexively, which sliced the kid's throat wide open. As his blood drained out swiftly, he stumbled to the floor. Goldie was in shock, watching as the young bear gasped his final breath.

"No!" Mama shouted.

She then charged furiously at Goldie, who straightened up and ran toward the mother bear. The girl buried the knife into the bear's abdomen and tackled her into Papa. All of them slammed hard into the nearest concrete wall. The impact enabled a secret function to unlock and open a section of the wall.

With the knife planted fatally deep in her torso, Mama collapsed dead to the floor while her husband plummeted down beside her, unconscious after his head whacked the cold, firm concrete. Goldie had no time to recover before facing a horror like nothing she had ever witnessed.

In a hidden room behind the now-open secret wall, a macabre, red glow in the space illuminated a morbid and gruesome array of furniture made of human body parts – a sofa upholstered in stretched skin, lamps made with severed heads, chairs constructed of blood-stained bones, a waterbed filled with blood, bile, and human organs.

The unbelievably grotesque sight struck her like a wrecking ball. She gagged onto the floor and felt a rush through her head. Her dream was over. No one was real, nothing was sacred. There was no comfort anywhere to be found. The grisly cache of mauled human remains in front of her summed it all up.

She took a step back, composed herself, and then scurried upstairs. Back in the kitchen, she hunted down a large, nearly full bottle of whiskey and a box of long matches. Marching back to the basement, she poured the booze all over the bears and whatever else she could in the room, including the human furniture. Then, she lit two matches and dropped them right onto the alcohol. The room was ablaze quickly.

She stared into the flames for a good, long minute, the orange and red flickers dancing devilishly on her worn, despondent face. As the fire grew fast, the girl recovered the bloody steak knife and left the basement. Tiredly, she then jogged out of the burning residence.

Goldie stood in front of the two blazing houses and dispiritedly watched the flames devour them bit by bit, chewing up her hopes, her dreams, any semblance of a life worth living.

A solid hour passed before the girl treaded back to the woods. She plopped down on the cool, moss-covered earth and sat up against a tall elm tree, allowing her tears to empty out of her like a faucet. After there were no more tears left to be cried, the girl took out the steak knife, wiped away the blood of her accidental victims, and did what she did best – cut herself.

However, this instrument was certainly much sharper than the convenience store razor she stole and normally used to compulsively cut herself. In fact, it was so sharp, it sliced open a major artery in her arm when she ran the blade swiftly and aggressively over her dirty, battered skin. It took no time at all for Goldie to bleed out and become the final casualty of this horrid night.

The chilled forest preserved her young corpse for a few nocturnal hours before a pack of ravenous foxes wandered through in the witching hour and made short work of it – a hearty meal to fill the unforgiving bellies of nature's night hunters. At morning's light, there was nothing more. Ashes to ashes, dust to dust.

Studying under esteemed writers Sonny Sykes and Charles McClelland, Bill Freas continued his education at West Chester University before he was hired in 2002 as the head writer of a TBS sketch-comedy pilot that ultimately did not make it to series. Subsequently, he optioned or sold over two dozen scripts, which included shorts, features, and pilots. As an author, he has written more than twenty published short stories, including three full collections. His produced credits as a writer span multiple genres and mediums. Currently, Bill also heads up Oceanicom Films' development department, where he oversees the development of US and international film and TV projects for the Australian company. Along with script, development, and production consultation, Bill is also a staff writer for Vancouver production company Foresight Entertainment, with which he has had an active partnership for over fifteen years.

EDGAR AND THE FAIRY

SUSAN E. ROGERS

Once upon a time, Edgar had a fairy. He named her Trilley because he couldn't repeat the discordant screech she spouted as the answer to his inquiry. He had been lonely, no mate or friends, but there was no doubt she belonged to him now. She followed him everywhere. Edgar hadn't a moment alone since she arrived six months ago, but he didn't mind. Nobody else he knew had a fairy.

Before Trilley, Edgar trudged to the woods each morning from his hut on the edge of the village. He gathered deadfall, twigs and limbs dropped by the trees to the forest floor, or mushrooms, careful to avoid the poisonous ones, and traded them to the villagers for what he needed to survive, cloth for patches when his breeches wore thin or flour to make his bread. His life never changed, day after day.

Where Trilley came from, Edgar never asked. She was invisible to everyone but him. Her figure was draped in shimmering gossamer. Her wings sparkled with green and purple bursts of light and made a soft whirring as she darted about, throwing kaleidoscopic waves of bouncing color over his pale bald head. She sang to him with squeals and shrills that clenched his teeth.

Anyone who saw them playing in the woods in the morning, or at his chores during the day, would certainly make a comment, but none did.

She was the size of a six-year-old, yet there was no weight to her as she sat on his shoulders. Sometimes she flitted around his head and the points of her ears raked through his hair or under his collar, leaving bloody scratches. She nuzzled his earlobes, tickling so he jerked his head away.

Once her pointy tooth got stuck and ripped a tear in the tender skin. His fingertips flew to the injury, but she nudged his hand away and lapped at the cut with her rough tongue. The nick healed instantly and she licked his fingers clean of the sticky red streaks. Edgar laughed.

Trilley often disappeared without warning, but always returned bringing Edgar a gift, some bauble or trinket. Once she brought him a gold ring with a fancy-cut gem, and another time a tiny hand mirror with a chime in the handle like a baby's toy. He kept all these gifts in a carved wooden chest in his bedroom.

The ring had dark spots that he thought were tarnish but they came off easily with a swipe of a cloth. Similar spots splattered a gold earring, but they were soft and squishy. Edgar didn't know what the drips were, but he wiped the earring clean and stowed it in the box.

He tried to find a gift to give her in return. His first few tries failed despite the folklore his mother had told. Trilley wanted nothing to do with sugar bread soaked in milk or swatches of soft velvet. Sweet-smelling bell-shaped flowers elicited no interest whatsoever. He shrugged and gave up. Trilley frowned.

Edgar usually ate soup made from the few vegetables he grew himself. Potatoes, carrots, and radishes were plentiful in his garden patch. One day when he gathered a particularly big load of firewood, he decided to trade it to the village butcher for a piece of venison, and discovered what Trilley really liked. He placed the steak on the table and went to look for his cleaver.

Before he could blink twice, she dove into the raw deer meat. Edgar watched in amazement as she slurped and chomped amid high-pitched moans of delight.

Finally, she lifted her head and looked at him.

Bits of venison clung to her face, and bloody juice ran from the corner of her mouth. She pointed at the bloody stain on the tabletop. When he shook his head, she shrieked and stomped her feet. Before he could react, her mouth clamped on his arm and her sharp teeth punctured his flesh.

Edgar yelped in pain and swatted her across the room. She flew out the window and disappeared.

She was gone for several days. Edgar had become used to his fairy being around, and he felt very lonely when he thought he'd never see her again. He watched at the window and sighed.

One night, he put out a plate of raw beef in hopes of luring her back. Two hours passed with no sign of Trilley, so he put the meat away and went to bed, heartbroken that his companion was gone for good.

In the middle of the night, something hard bounced off his head. He woke with a start and turned on the light. A small twig lay on the pillow next to him. He picked it up and turned it over and around to get a good look. Four inches long, brown and dried, a smooth scar at the base, it looked rather like a finger with wrinkles where the knuckles would be and a knot at the tip that resembled a nail.

A high-pitched cackle greeted him as he put the stick in his wooden box. He grinned to see Trilley floating near the ceiling. He ran to the kitchen and got the meat for her. She laughed and clapped and devoured every last shred. She planted a bloody kiss on his bald head, then licked it clean. He went back to bed and slept soundly for the rest of the night.

When morning came, Edgar got up and stumbled to his hands and knees. He tried to stand, but something was wrong with his feet. When he managed to sit upright, he saw that both his big toes were missing. In their place were patches of nicely healed pink skin over the stumps, as if the toes were never there. He looked around for Trilley, but she was nowhere to be seen.

He crawled to the carved chest and took out the child's toy mirror. He howled when he saw his nose and one ear were missing. The buzz of Trilley's wings sounded behind him. She screeched so loud that the mirror shattered. Edgar slid down the front of the cabinet as the fairy approached with her mouth wide and her pointy teeth bared. The shrill shriek of her song rose higher and higher.

Blood trickled between his fingers as Edgar clapped his hands over his ears to block out the noise. Snot and blood gushed from his nose. His eyeballs burst. He slumped over as his heart exploded inside his chest.

Trilley's shriek subsided to squeals of laughter at the sight of bloody Edgar on the floor. She grabbed the wooden chest with her trinkets and flew away.

Susan E. Rogers lives in sunny St. Pete Beach, Florida, USA transplanted from Massachusetts. Her move was the catalyst to focus on her life-long ambition to write. Her other interests include genealogy and psychic spirituality, and she often twists these into her writing. She self-published her first book in 2018 about her own psychic experiences, and published an occult thriller with an indie press in Sept. 2023. A supernatural mystery novel is under contract with another publisher for a planned release in 2024. Starting in 2020, her short fiction has been published in print anthologies and several literary and genre magazines, including Cobra Milk Literary, Bluing the Blade, Luna Station Quarterly, Nightmare Narratives, and Horror Tree's Trembling with Fear.

DUCK

DAVID E. ANDERSON

As Heather Jamison slowly regained consciousness, disoriented and with a terrible pain in her skull, she fought to remember what had happened. A sense of impending doom filled her when she realized her hands were bound and that she was lying on something cold and solid.

Fragments of her memory began to slide together. She remembered the three men chasing her through the woods with feral grins. Two carried axes and the other a club, maybe an old baseball bat. She'd been out for a hike, and saw them cresting a hill, howling and yapping. She'd turned and ran, but they were relentless and closed in on her.

Then everything went black.

Opening her eyes, Heather found herself strapped to a table in what appeared to be a decrepit dining room. The house was a nightmare of rotting wood and filthy drywall, a place where hope had withered long ago.

She raised her head and saw her hands were bound with rough rope, looped around her waist. Three thick, black straps pinned her down. They looked like the tie-downs for cars, constricting her legs, hips and upper chest. Escape seemed impossible.

The room appeared empty, but from outside came the unsettling sounds of voices and the rhythmic thud of an axe splitting wood.

"Hey, there," said a voice—feminine and friendly.

Startled, Heather looked around and spotted a

girl, no more than ten, with choppy brown hair and a slightly plump frame, sitting on a wooden chair and watching her curiously. The girl wore blue jeans with ripped-out knees and a white shirt that was much too big and badly stained.

Another whack of the axe made Heather jump.

"They're outside," the girl said.

"Who's outside?" Heather asked, her voice trembling.

The girl hesitated, looking left and right, as if about to reveal a dark secret. "My dad and my uncles. Hank and Chris. They're the ones who took you."

Heather considered asking what the plans were for her, but she was also pretty sure she didn't want to know. She was panicked enough as it was, her heart threatening to pound out of her chest. She didn't need details.

"What are they doing out there?" she asked.

"Preparing the fire pit," the girl replied with a chilling calm. "They're going to cook you, and we're all going to eat you."

Heather let out a slight whine. These people weren't just ordinary psychopaths; they were cannibals. Some kind of demented freaks who split off from society long ago, hiding out in these deep woods.

"It's what we do," said the girl. "It's...it's who we are."

Heather looked at the girl. Other than her clothing and haircut, she looked like a normal kid. Those men had deformed heads and sunken eye sockets. She could believe the men were brothers, but no way was she the child of any one of them.

Heather tried to keep her voice steady. "What's your name?"

"Duck," said the girl.

"Your name is Duck?"

"Well, that's what they call me. My real name is Dorothy. But they don't call me Dorothy, just Duck."

"Can I call you Duck, Duck?" Heather forced a smile, her mind racing. This girl was different than the men, somehow, and could end up being her only chance of not ending up cooked in the fire pit.

"Sure," said Duck. "What's your name?"

"Heather. Look, Duck, I can see you're not like them. You don't want to be here, right? You don't like eating people, do you?"

Duck shrugged. "I'm not like them," she said. "I think I'm...adopted."

Heather couldn't picture those three brutes going through an adoption agency. They took her—stole her. Maybe intending to cook and eat her, but then had some kind of a change of heart. Since Duck clearly didn't remember, it had to have been when she was quite young.

Then, a memory entered her head: the stories on the news, the posters. It must have been about seven years ago…

"What did you say your name was, Duck? Your real name?"

"Dorothy," she replied, her eyes narrowing in suspicion.

"Dorothy...Swan?"

Duck stood up from the chair, surprise on her face.

"How old are you, Dorothy?" Heather asked.

"Nine."

"My God. You are. You're Dorothy Swan. I remember that. I was fifteen when you disappeared, so that was…seven years ago. These people aren't your family. Your family—"

Footsteps from the kitchen interrupted her.

A short, stocky woman, dressed in the same ragged clothing, entered the room. She gazed at Heather with fury.

"Duck?" asked the woman, her voice dripping with menace, not taking her eyes off their visitor.

"Yes, Ma?" Duck replied sheepishly, lowering her head.

"Go play outside, and let me talk to our guest," she ordered.

Duck scurried away, leaving Ma alone with Heather.

"There's a reward," Heather blurted out. "Fifty thousand dollars, I think. Maybe more than that. You could really fix this place up, get some—"

"She's not Dorothy Swan," said the woman.

"Duck is my daughter. Birthed her myself. Don't go putting crazy ideas into her head."

"I'm sorry," Heather said, feigning regret. "My mistake."

"Don't ever speak of it again," said the woman, stepping closer. "You're a guest in our house, and—"

Heather felt something inside her burst, her anger spilling out. "Guest?" She struggled against the straps. "Do I look like a guest, you crazy bitch?"

The woman slapped Heather across her face with an open palm, her eyes blazing with fury. "Shut your filthy mouth!"

Heather glanced toward the kitchen, hoping Duck was still nearby and listening. "The Swan family loves their Dorothy very much," she said, ignoring the flaring pain in her cheek. "They live nearby, in Marietta, and desperately want her back. You have to..."

The woman slapped her again, even harder.

Heather's words echoed in Duck's mind. The name "Dorothy Swan" tugged at the edges of her memory. She remembered a yard, a mansion, a loving family, a mom with beautiful eyes, a dad with a goofy smile, a life far removed from this nightmare.

Her new "family" never called her Dorothy, just Duck. That name was solely from her memory, and Swan rang a bell. Yes, she was nearly certain her name was Dorothy Swan. She needed to get back to them: her real family. Whatever it took, she was going back.

She'd remained in the kitchen, and her eyes now settled on a large butcher knife. Surely Ma would be using it on Heather, with whom she was still arguing and providing yet another slap.

Duck seized the knife, her hands trembling, and crept forward, clutching the wooden handle tightly in her small hands. She had one shot at this. If Ma saw her and got the knife away, there'd be hell to pay. She might even end up in the fire pit. She quietly stepped back into the dining room.

She focused her eyes on Ma's back, then lunged forward, driving the knife between Ma's shoulder blades with a grunt.

Oh, Ma's screams were deafening, and blood spurted from around the edges of the blade lodged in her back.

"Help me, Duck!" the woman gasped, spitting blood as she did so. Clearly, she did not realize it was her daughter who'd assaulted her.

Duck dove under the table, working frantically to free Heather from the straps.

She could hear the men coming, their heavy footsteps approaching the house, and their voices calling for Ma, who had now fallen to the floor with a thud.

Duck managed to free the middle strap, and Heather maneuvered her legs out from the lowest strap while Duck unhooked the upper one.

Heather climbed off of the table, her hands still bound around her waist, but there was no time to worry about that. The men were approaching the front door.

"Come on, Duck," she urged, stepping through the pool of blood and heading into the kitchen and towards the back door.

"No," Duck insisted, stopping Heather in her tracks. "I'll just slow you down. Go, get help. I'll stop them."

Heather nodded, her heart aching at the idea of leaving the poor kid behind, but knowing Duck was right. "I'll send someone for you," she promised, and disappeared out the back door.

The men burst into the dining room to see that

their dinner had fled and that their matriarch lay dead on the floor.

"Wha...what happened?" asked her Uncle Hank.

"She… She stabbed…Ma. She…" Duck stammered, pointing to the back door. "Get that bitch!"

Their faces twisted with rage, they charged out the back. All were unarmed, except for Uncle Chris, who had an axe.

Duck knew Heather didn't stand a chance. Even without Duck slowing her down, she'd have to evade these three men for miles, and that wasn't going to happen. They already caught her once; they'd catch her again.

Duck slipped out the front door and ran off into the woods. She had no idea where she was going, except that she was going in the opposite direction of her so-called "dad" and uncles. All she knew was that with the men distracted and Ma dead, this was the perfect time to escape.

It was well after night fell that Duck found a road.

A family stopped and picked her up, taking her into town to the police station. She told the police her name was Dorothy Swan, and her family was contacted. They were there within minutes, weeping with joy as they embraced their long-lost daughter.

Blood was taken from Dorothy and her parents for a DNA test to confirm Dorothy's identity. The results wouldn't be determined until the next day, but with the family certain they had found their daughter, they let them take her home.

The DNA tests confirmed her identity, and on the same day, the FBI raided the house in the woods. The men resisted, and a violent battle ensued. All three men were killed, and the remains of nine missing people, including Heather Jamison, were discovered, with many more suspected to have been devoured over almost three decades.

Dorothy's return was celebrated with a grand party at their mansion, and she vowed to forget the "Duck" name and the nightmare of her life in the woods. She managed, but only for a while.

After a few months, Duck was found in the kitchen, having killed and cut up her three-year-old brother, Eric, trying to cook his legs in the family's oven.

David E. Anderson grew up in the '70s, loving Godzilla movies and the "Night Stalker" series, developing a love for horror early on. As a teenager, he immersed himself in the books by the likes of Stephen King, F. Paul Wilson and Dean Koontz, and wanted to try his hand at what they do so well. He wrote his first novel, "The Void," in his mid-teens, followed by six more—three of which he's self-published.

THE CLOCKWORK CHILDREN

MARIE LESTRANGE

D amp fog oozed through the streets of London like pus from a festering wound, infecting every crack and crevice. Gas lamps sputtered like dying fireflies, their sickly light hardly piercing the thick blanket of blindness. Halos of jaundiced yellow hung in the miasma, more a mockery of illumination than any real comfort against the encroaching dark. Two small figures darted between the shadows of this twilight world, their ragged clothes hanging off of them like loose skin.

Hansel and Gretel, orphaned and hollowed by hunger, moved with the twitchy desperation of feral street cats. Soot caked their faces, dark masks that spoke of endless hours crawling through chimneys, their lungs no doubt filled with the same grimy residue that coated their skin.

"Move it, Gretel!" Hansel whispered with a harsh rasp. They flattened themselves against a crumbling wall as a constable's heavy tread echoed nearby. The siblings held their breath, hearts pounding like the relentless pistons that powered the city.

If they were discovered…to the workhouse they'd go. T'was a prison of enforced labor and crushed spirits—much worse than their current engagement.

The clack of footsteps on cobblestone faded. Gretel's cold and corpse-like fingers found Hansel's. "We need to find somewhere to stay tonight," she murmured. "The night's teeth are getting sharper."

Hansel nodded, worry etched into his face like acid on metal. "Old Tom mentioned a warehouse.

Might find a dry corner to curl up in, if we're lucky."

They set off again, weaving through the labyrinth of streets like rats in a maze. Grand houses loomed above them, windows glowing with warmth and laughter that felt as unreachable and unfamiliar as the stars hidden behind the smog. In the distance, factory chimneys belched acrid smoke, feeding the ever-hungry maw of progress.

The stench of the river hit them like a physical blow—a noxious cocktail of sewage, chemicals, and decay. Their stomachs growled in unison, a hollow ache that gnawed at their insides, but sadly it was a sensation they'd grown accustomed to.

As they neared the warehouse district, a pulsing light caught their attention. It writhed in the distance, casting elongated shadows that danced and twisted like tortured souls.

"What on God's green earth is that?" Gretel

breathed, her curiosity overriding the exhaustion and cold.

Hansel squinted. "It's coming from that hill. Look—there's some kind of building up there."

As they drew ever closer, the fog thinned, revealing a sight that unhinged their jaws. Perched atop the hill was a mansion born of a fever dream. Grotesque spires twisted skyward, their architecture twisted…distorted… reaching towards the heavens like the grasping fingers of a madman's fevered nightmare. Vast windows pulsed with that same otherworldly light, while gears and pistons adorned the outer walls in a mechanical cancer.

"It's... beautiful," Gretel gasped.

Hansel nodded, equally transfixed. "And definitely warm. Maybe... maybe they'd let us sleep in the stables?"

As they approached the gates, a figure material-
ized from the mist, seemingly from nowhere, but reason said she had to have been standing there the whole
time.

Right?

She was tall and rail-thin, with frizzy, unkempt
hair the color of tarnished silver and eyes that glowed
an unnatural green. Gears and cogs seemed to writhe
beneath the bombazine fabric of her dress like para-
sites.

"Well, well," the tall woman's voice dripped
with saccharine sweetness, a mystical tone that sent
shivers down the spine. "What have we here? Two little
chimney sweeps, far from their sooty nests?"

Hansel instinctively stepped in front of Gretel to
shield her, but his sister spoke up, her frail voice small
yet determined. "Please, ma'am. We're sorry to trouble
you, but we have nowhere else to go. Might we sleep

in your stables? We'll be gone by morning, we swear."

The woman's lips curled into a smile that didn't quite reach her eyes. "My dears, I couldn't possibly allow that. Far too cold for little birds like you to roost in stables."

Gretel hung her head, embarrassed to have even asked.

The tall woman paused to study them, her brass monocle whirring as it adjusted. Then she smiled. "I am Dr. Greta Sweetmann, and this is my home. Why don't you come inside? I have warm beds and hot food to spare."

Hansel and Gretel exchanged a look. Kindness like this was as rare as gold in their world, and they had learned far too young to be wary of adults bearing gifts.

The promise of warmth and food...a real meal, not like the scraps they usually had, beckoned like a steam whistle signaling the end of a shift.

Clasping hands, Hansel and Gretel nodded.

Dr. Sweetmann led them through gates that hissed shut behind them. With each step closer, they got a clearer view of the mechanical monstrosities that infested every surface of her home. Clockwork birds chirped from metal trees, their songs discordant and wrong. Steam-powered fountains gurgled and spat, the water an oily black.

"Welcome to my humble abode." Dr. Sweetmann's pride dripped from her every word. "I'm a scientist, you see, always pushing the boundaries of what's possible." Her smile wilted, ever so slightly. "But science can be such lonely work. It would be a delight to have some young minds around to... nurture."

As they entered the vast foyer, with its twisting staircases and whirring contraptions, Hansel and Gretel felt a whirring of something rather unfamiliar. It wasn't the hunger in their bellies or fear of being taken off the streets and imprisoned...it was a flicker of hope.

Perhaps their luck had finally changed. Perhaps... they had found not just shelter for a night, but a true home.

***

The next few days passed in a surreal haze. Dr. Sweetmann clothed them in fabrics that felt wrong against their skin, like someone would surely come crashing through the gigantic front doors and accuse them of stealing them. She fed them meals so rich their shrunken tummies rebelled, and gave them beds so soft they felt like they were drowning among the fine cotton. Each room held a new wonder to explore, the whirring and buzzing and clicking of machinery becoming a familiar and comforting sound.

The sound of...home.

In the library, books fluttered on steam-powered wings, their pages rustling like a symphony of hissing pipes, and clanking gears came from the kitchen, machines producing meals that looked more like abstract art than food. Even the bathrooms were a nightmare of twisting pipes that seemed to pulse with a life of their own.

Hansel and Gretel had never experienced anything like it.

Dr. Sweetmann insisted upon tutoring them, force-feeding their minds with knowledge that felt sharp and dangerous. Hansel showed an aptitude for mechanics, his fingers dancing over gears and levers with an almost feverish intensity. Gretel absorbed everything like a sponge, her quick mind making connections that sometimes made Dr. Sweetmann's eyes glitter with pride.

"You two are remarkable children," the doctor

would often say, her gaze fixed upon them with un-wavering intensity, as if cataloging every minute detail for future reference. "So much potential, just waiting to be... unlocked."

Yet, as the days bled into one another, things felt off. Felt…wrong, like the silken clothing, began to seep through the cracks of their newfound paradise. In the dead of night, they would hear things that set their teeth on edge– a grinding sound that mimicked a rake being dragged across a marble floor…or the hiss of escaping steam that sounded too much like screams.

"Just my machines settling," Dr. Sweetmann would say with a wave of her bony hand, but again, her eyes told a different story than the smile welded to her face. "Nothing to trouble yourselves over, my little birds."

Gretel noticed the locked doors, the half-answers, the way some of the mansion's automata seemed to watch them with an intelligence that made her uncomfortable.

Hansel, lost in his mechanical studies, was slower to sense the wrongness, but even he couldn't ignore the occasional unexplained movements of machines that he glimpsed from the corner of his eye.

One evening, as they ate in the opulent dining room, their favorite room in the house, Gretel's curiosity finally overcame her growing dread.

"Dr. Sweetmann," she whispered, "why did you really take us in? Surely a great scientist like yourself has more important things to do than look after two orphans."

The doctor's fork paused halfway to her mouth, and for a heartbeat, something dark and hungry flickered behind her eyes. Yet it was gone so quickly that it had surely only been a trick of the flickering light.

"My dear Gretel." Dr. Sweetmann's voice was thick as the honey from the mountains. "You and your brother are far more important than you realize. You see, I believe that children—bright, adaptable children like yourselves—are the key to the future. My work... our work together...will change the world. You'll see."

As she spoke, a grandfather clock in the corner chimed. Its mechanical figures emerged to dance their eternal waltz, but to Gretel's horror, one of them turned its head to look directly at her. Its tiny metal face twisted in a silent scream, eyes pleading for a release from the clock that would never come.

And in this moment, Dr. Sweetmann's mansion suddenly felt like a cage—a cage with two little birds trapped inside.

As weeks bled into a grotesque game of pretend normality, the mansion's clockwork bowels churned with a clearly malevolent purpose. Hansel, his mind dulled by the allure of scientific wonder, ignored the wrongness that seeped from every gear and piston.

But not Gretel. No, no. She felt the weight of unseen eyes boring into her skull, her dreams plagued by the whirring of unnatural machines.

***

One night, sleep eluding her, much the same as peace did within these walls, Gretel's bare feet skimmed the cold floors as she crept through corridors that, at times, seemed to breathe. The ever-present ticking of countless clocks formed a hellish percussion, each beat bringing with it a sense of impending doom.

And then…a shadow darted across the light.

Someone was here! Someone to save them!

The burn of hysteria crawled up Gretel's throat as a misshapen figure scuttled across the far end of the hall, its movements a jerky and crude imitation of humanity. It vanished into shadow with a sound like grinding bone.

"Hello?" Her voice trembled, barely a whisper in the oppressive silence.

The darkness answered with a bone-chilling wail, a sound of such profound anguish it teetered on the edge of madness.

She wasn't sure why, but curiosity drove her forward to find the maker of the moan. Her foot struck something, and she bent to find a small brass cog. It was warm, actually almost hot, and smeared with something dark and viscous. The smell of rust and salt filled her nostrils.

Too many years on the streets had taught her what that smell was.

Blood.

A crash shattered the silence she stalled in. Gretel took it as her signal to run, her heart a frenzied drumbeat. As she dove beneath sweat-soaked sheets, a wrong voice—Dr. Sweetmann's, yet twisted into something vile—snarled from the darkness: "You fool! They mustn't see you yet!"

***

Morning light did nothing to dispel the horrors of the night before. Gretel thrust the bloodied cog into Hansel's hands, her eyes wide and red from hardly any sleep.

How could she sleep comfortably in this house of unseen horrors?

"Something's wrong here, Hansel. Terribly wrong. I think...I think she's doing something bad."

Hansel frowned, turning the cog over in a now trembling hand. "Maybe it's just part of an experiment? She is a scientist, after all."

"The blood, Hansel!" Gretel hissed. "And that... that thing I saw. It wasn't natural. It wasn't human."

Before Hansel could respond, Dr. Sweetmann's voice sliced through the air like a clockwork blade, making them both flinch. "Ah, there you are, my dears! I have a special treat for you today. How would you like to assist me in my laboratory?"

As they followed the doctor's swaying form through twisting passages, Gretel's gaze fixed on the woman's right hand. With each step, it twitched and whirred, fingers flexing with mechanical precision. Beneath her dress sleeve, something pulsed and writhed, as if her very veins were filled with tiny, squirming gears.

The laboratory door swung open with the groan of tortured metal, revealing a chamber that stretched endlessly into shadow. Bubbling vats lined the walls, their contents roiling with surely nothing good inside.

Electrical apparatus crackled and spat, arcs of blue-white energy dancing between copper coils– but it was the glass tanks that drew their gaze and turned their stomachs to ice.

Children near their age floated in murky fluid, suspended in a nightmarish limbo between flesh and machine. Some of them had mechanical limbs, twisted and grafted to torn flesh, while others were little more than brains encased in macabre clockwork shells. All of them twitched and pulsed with a horrid attempt at mimicking life, their faces frozen in expressions of agony or rapture.

"Beautiful, aren't they?" Dr. Sweetmann's voice dripped with her usual saccharine sweetness, her eyes flickering with madness. "The future of humanity, the perfect fusion of mankind and machine!"

Gretel stumbled backward, the burn of anxiety mixed with bile rising in her throat. Hansel stood transfixed, his mind struggling to process the abominations before him.

"You're...experimenting on children?" Hansel's voice was a strangled whisper.

Dr. Sweetmann turned to them and for the first time, they saw the true horror lurking behind her eyes. "Experimenting? Oh no, my dears. I'm perfecting them. Freeing these children from the weaknesses of flesh, making them stronger, better." She grinned wickedly.

"The same as I will do for you."

As she spoke, her voice deepened, morphing into a mechanical rasp. Her very form began to twist and writhe, gears and pistons erupting from beneath her skin in a sickening symphony of tearing flesh and grinding metal.

Where the innocent-looking Dr. Sweetmann had stood moments before, there was now a monstrous fusion of woman and machine, her face split in a grin of steel and bloody sinew.

"You see," the former Dr. Sweetmann growled, steam hissing from joints in her neck, "I am my own greatest success. But the process... created something new within me. Something stronger, something unbound by the foolish morals of the common man. You may call this persona Hyde, as like the doctor of legend, I too have split my soul to pursue greatness!"

Hansel's fingers closed around Gretel's wrist, yanking her towards the door. "Run!" he shouted, but the mechanical monsters were faster. Metal arms shot out to stop them, ensnaring the children in a grip that threatened to crush their feeble, human bones.

As they struggled against their captors, Dr. Sweetmann—or rather, the Hyde persona—loomed over them. "Don't fret, my little ones," she crooned, her voice a horrific blend of maternal affection and mechanical hunger. "Soon, you'll be perfect too. And together, we'll remake this weak, fleshy world in our image!"

Hansel and Gretel's screams echoed through the mansion's iron halls as they were dragged deeper into the nightmarish laboratory. The door slammed shut with the finality of a coffin lid, sealing them in a world where the line between flesh and machine blurred into meaninglessness.

To Be Continued…

Author of the Crimson Cobblestones, Dr. Marie Lestrange is an artist, musician and special educator with a particular interest in Historical Horror. She draws outrageous ABC books for adults and interviews Indie Horror authors on her Moths to the Flame podcast every Tuesday night. Lestrange also serves as the chairman of the Horror Writers Association Tennessee Chapter and CEO of CCM/Sinister Society. She's afraid of most things, but chickens are the worst! You can find her (too frequently) online on her various socials @linktr.ee/lestrangebooks

Want More From The

SINISTER SOCIETY?

Follow along on our social medias
@sinistersociety

&

Join our Facebook Group for submissions calls and latest updates!
https://www.facebook.com/groups/1444531013102495